THE HOUSE OF DIES DREAR

The House of Dies Drear

VIRGINIA HAMILTON

A TRUMPET CLUB SPECIAL EDITION

The excerpt on page 198 from Paul Laurence Dunbar's
"We Wear the Mask" is quoted with the permission of
Dodd, Mead & Company, publishers of *The Complete
Poems of Paul Laurence Dunbar.*

Published by The Trumpet Club
1540 Broadway, New York, New York 10036

ISBN 0-440-84696-X

This edition published by arrangement with
Macmillan Publishing Company

Printed in the United States of America
March 1993

10 9 8 7 6 5 4
OPM

FOR ARNOLD,

   who loves mystery most of all

chapter 1

THOMAS dreamed he
walked a familiar forest, following a time-
worn path of the Tuscaroras. The trail seemed
the same as he had known it all his life.
The way he walked it, without making any
sound, was true to the way ancient Indian
braves had walked it. But now the once
familiar evergreens on either side were gi-
gantic. Their needles were as large as railroad spikes. He had no trouble accepting the
great new height of the trees or the long,
smooth size of the needles. It was the awful
smell of resin and oil over everything that
upset him. The odor nearly choked him; the
trees gave it off, as though they were raining
turpentine. He seemed to feel it on his hair
and on his hands. His palms itched and his
eyes burned. He tried to get the smell out of

his mind and stopped on the path to cut an enormous branch from a fallen pine.

He made tiny marks on the bark with one of his whittling tools, and he didn't find it unusual to be using so small an instrument for such hard work. He'd always used whittling tools to cut branches. He had started whistling to himself when a man swung down from a mile-high spruce.

"Stay back," the man said. He lifted the huge branch Thomas wanted and flung it away as if it were nothing.

Thomas stood still. He began to feel small. "Papa says you will do," he told the man, "but I don't say it. We are going anyway."

"Carolina is for you," the man said. "Stay back." He reached for Thomas with arms covered with curls of white hair. His eyes glowed red and then spewed fire.

Thomas leaped for a tall pair of stilts against a tree. Fastening them to his legs, he turned around on the path.

"I'm running," he said. But when he moved, the stilts sank into the bed of over-sized pine needles covering the ground.

The man grabbed Thomas' ankles. Thomas fell slowly forward from a long way up. He could hear the wind whistling by his ears as he fell.

I'll never reach the end of the trail, he thought. And for the first time, he was afraid.

Thomas Small lurched out of this dream, waking his twin brothers at the same time. The boys leaned against him and looked at him with wide, senseless eyes. Thomas didn't dare move. His heart pounded as the dream fear moved up and down his back. He couldn't think where he was.

In a few minutes, the twins were sleeping again. Thomas could rearrange them and rest his arms.

That was a good dream. Good and scary, he thought. I was in the trees at home and the man was somebody I should know. I can't place him right now, but I do know him.

He glanced out of the car window and smiled. He knew where he was now and everything was fine. The day was a dismal Saturday; the month was March. All around were heavy patches of mist, and there was a steady rain. His papa's sedan with the red trailer attached was the lone automobile on the Blue Ridge Mountain Highway. Thomas was thirteen years old today and never in his life had he been so far from home.

Home, he thought. Well, I'm sorry.

He and his family were leaving an old house and folks who were mostly relatives. He had known the old house and the old people forever.

"Like Great-grandmother Jeffers," he said

to himself. His papa had asked Great-grand-mother to come with them to live. Thomas recalled how she'd been leaning on her bright blue gate at the time.

No longer was there a fence around Great-grandmother Jeffers' house. Its blue pickets had long since fallen and rotted back into the ground. But the gate continued to stand, and Thomas, since the age of ten, had painted it bright blue every spring.

Great-grandmother had laughed when his father asked her to come with them. Her hand was propped under her chin as she leaned heavily on that old gate.

"You go look at the North two, three times," she had said to his papa. "Then come back here one day and tell me if it is better."

"I'll tell you now," his papa had said. "It won't be worse." He had smiled and kissed Great-grandmother. No need to tell her to take care of herself. She always had. He turned and walked swiftly away.

Thomas had stayed a moment. "Who will keep your gate?" he had asked her. "Who will paint it each spring?"

"You think you are the only boy in all these parts that can paint my gate?" she had asked him.

"I'm the only one who ever has," Thomas had said.

"Well, that's so," she had answered. She

looked at Thomas hard. "You can trot back here next spring and paint it again, if you've a mind to. Spring," she said softly. "That's a long row to hoe."

Thomas saw something in her eyes that made him feel sad. But then whatever it had been was gone. She'd looked at him with that mean expression she used only with him and the bobwhite quail that lived off her handouts. He had to smile, for he knew she liked him even better than the bobwhite.

"I've got to go now," she had said. "No telling what fool thought took hold of your papa to leave these hills to go live in some craven house. I'm going to fix my chicory. I expect I'll roast it all night and all day tomorrow. Maybe then your papa will get you all there in one piece." She believed roasting chicory was the best power to ward off calamity. Thomas accepted the fact and was comforted.

Great-grandmother had turned and, not looking back, slowly walked to her house. At the steps, she held up her arm in a wave. Thomas hadn't needed to say anything. Within the wave was everything between them.

Thomas had few children to play with in those mountains he and his family were leaving. Homes were sometimes foothills apart. Most of the families with boys Thomas' age had already gone away North. No one heard from them again and old people like Great-grandmother Jeffers took this to be a sign that the North was a place of sorrow. Still Thomas hadn't minded being alone most of the time. There had been the forest to walk and there had been Great-grandmother to talk to.

He stared out of the car window and thought about the trees spreading up and over the hills behind his old home. There were times when he had sensed a coming rain and raced it to the pines. Diving under heavy branches, he had watched the rain slant into the forest. It never reached where he lay sheltered, but from the tree's farthest boughs made a silver circle around him.

"I won't think about it again," he promised himself. "It'll be fun living somewhere in Ohio." They were to live in a big house, and only his father had seen it.

Thomas sat wondering why it was taking them so long to get there.

Maybe an axle will break, he thought. Maybe we'll run out of gas in the night, with woods on both sides of the road!

If that happened, he would creep through the darkness in search of a house. And at last he would see ghostly lights flickering through the trees.

If it's going to take forever, we might as well have some excitement, he thought.

"Papa," he said suddenly, "tell about the new house again."

His father drove hunched over the steering wheel of the car. When Thomas broke the silence, Mr. Small took up a cloth to wipe the windshield. Then he rubbed the cloth on the back of his neck. He was tired of driving and tired of the rain that had stayed with them since morning. Yet he hadn't changed his plan to reach the new house by this afternoon at the latest.

"How many times must I tell it to you before you get it all?" he asked Thomas.

"Just once more, Papa," said Thomas. He had the story straight after the first time he heard it. He simply liked the tone of his papa's voice whenever he spoke about anything so full of history as the new house in Ohio.

"Well," his father began, "it has gables and eaves and pillars. It's large, quite large. There are many windows from floor to ceiling and there's a veranda all the way around on the outside."

"It must look like a plantation house," Thomas said. He pictured a gold mansion with green trim and a lawn as long as forever.

"No, not *quite* like that," said Mr. Small,

smiling. "Not that stately. Our place is more
. . . more . . . well . . ." he hesitated.

". . . more sinister," Mrs. Small finished
for him.

Neither Thomas nor his father had realized that Mrs. Small was awake. For most of
the morning's journey, she'd slept in the
front seat with her head cradled on a pillow.
Now she shivered and sighed. "How I could
let myself get talked into this!" she said.
"Going off to live somewhere I've never seen.
Rattling around in a big old place!"

"You're just as excited about going as
Papa and me," Thomas said. He leaned
forward against the front seat and looked
sideways at his mother. He liked the way she
almost smiled when he teased her. "I don't
think she'll like walking in the rain much
anymore though, Papa," he said.

His father laughed, and his mother had to
laugh, too. No, she didn't like so much rain.
That was why she'd slept so long. She didn't
like thinking about a big Civil War house
she had never laid eyes on. It had been an
important station on the Underground Railroad, and Thomas still wanted to hear about
it, even if his mother didn't.

"Does the house look haunted?" he asked.

Mr. Small was a long time answering. He
finally shrugged. "It's a handsome place, once
you get used to it," he said. "A fine period

piece. It will be the talk of the whole town once I have it painted and landscaped properly."

"What's the town like?" Thomas asked.

"Oh, it's like any small village," Mr. Small said. "And like most Ohio towns, it has a good college at one end of it. But our house isn't in the town, Thomas."

"I thought it was," said Thomas.

"No, it sits alone on a rise in a kind of wilderness." His father spoke then to Mrs. Small. "I believe the townspeople thought I was out of my mind when I finally signed that lease."

Thomas heard caution come into his father's voice. "I never did get the complete floor plans from the real estate people—did I tell you that? They said the plans had been missing for years. They've no idea how many hidden rooms and such the house has. We do have the partial plans though. I should be able to puzzle the whole of it out from them. But it's odd, don't you think, that all the complete plans should be gone?"

"That should tell you there's something funny about that house and anything to do with it," Mrs. Small said.

Thomas' father cleared his throat loudly and gave Mrs. Small a warning glance. But Thomas had heard what she said and he let his mother's words pass into his mind in a neat line. He would think about them some other time. Right now, he was thinking about the new house sitting alone.

"I do wish the rain would stop before we reach that place," Mrs. Small said. She shivered again and tied her scarf tighter about her neck.

"Papa . . ." Thomas said, "does 'wilderness' mean the soil is dead and trees can't grow? Does it mean there's no hope left in the land?"

"What a funny thing to think of!" said Mrs. Small.

"I did say the house stood alone," Mr. Small said. "Thomas was thinking of that."

"No, I was thinking about North Carolina and Great-grandmother," said Thomas. "I was thinking that Great-grandmother and all the other old people had lived in wilderness just forever almost. Maybe that's why she wouldn't come with us. Maybe she thought she was only changing one wilderness for another."

Mr. Small was silent for a time. "Some folks might think a hundred-mile stretch of pine was wilderness," he said, "although you wouldn't, Thomas, because you grew up in pine country. And some might call the prairie wilderness, but I suspect it must have looked pretty good to the pioneer. No, I meant by 'wilderness' that the house itself has about it an atmosphere of desolation."

"But you say it's by a town," said Thomas.

"Yes," Mr. Small said.

"And you say it sits alone."

"Absolutely alone," Mr. Small answered. "There's no way to describe the feel of it or its relation to the town. You have to see it and know about it that way."

"I wish we'd hurry and get there," Thomas said. "It feels like we've been riding forever."

They lapsed into silence. Thomas could think of no better birthday present than to have the new house suit him. He wanted to like it in the same way he liked the masses of clouds in front of a storm or the dark wood of the pine forest back home.

His father had given him a book for his birthday. It was a volume, bound in real leather, about the Civil War, the Underground Railroad and slaves. Thomas loved the smell of real leather, and he rubbed the book lightly back and forth beneath his nose. Then he leaned back, flipping idly through the pages. In a moment his brothers were nestled against him, but Thomas did not even notice.

He had come across a curious piece of information earlier. Of the one hundred thousand slaves who fled from the South to Can-

ada between 1810 and 1850, forty thousand
of them had passed through Ohio. Thomas
didn't know why this fact surprised him, yet
it did. He knew a lot about slaves. His father
had taught Civil War history in North Carolina. He would be teaching it in Ohio in the
very town in which they were going to live.
He had taught Thomas even more history
than Thomas cared to know. Thomas knew
that Elijah Anderson had been the "superin-
tendent" of the Underground Railroad in
Ohio and that he had finally died in prison
in Kentucky. He knew that in the space of
seven years, one thousand slaves had died in
Kentucky. But the fact that forty thousand
escaping slaves had fled through Ohio started
him thinking.

Ohio will be my new home, he thought. A
lot of those slaves must have stayed in Ohio
because Canada was farther than they could
have believed. Or they had liked Elijah Anderson so much, they'd just stayed with
him. Or maybe once they saw the Ohio
River, they thought it was the Jordan and
that the Promised Land lay on the other side.

The idea of exhausted slaves finding the
Promised Land on the banks of the Ohio
River pleased Thomas. He'd never seen the
Ohio River, but he could clearly imagine
freed slaves riding horses up and down its
slopes. He pictured the slaves living in great

communities as had the Iroquois, and they
had brave leaders like old Elijah Anderson.

"Papa . . ." Thomas said.

"Yes, Thomas," said Mr. Small.

"Do you ever wonder if any runaway slaves
from North Carolina went to Ohio?"

Mr. Small was startled by the question. He
laughed and said, "You've been reading the
book I gave you. I'm glad, it's a good book.
I'm sure some slaves fled from North Carolina.
They escaped from all over the South, and
it's likely that half of them passed through
Ohio on their way to Canada."

Thomas sank back into his seat, arranging
his sprawling brothers against him. He
smoothed his hand over the book and had
half a mind to read it from cover to cover.
He would wake the twins and read it all to
them. They loved for him to read aloud,
even though they couldn't understand very
much.

No, thought Thomas. They are tired from
being up late last night. They will only cry.

Thomas' brothers were named Billy and
Buster and they knew all sorts of things.
Once Thomas had taken up a cotton ball just
to show them about it. They understood right
away what it was. They had turned toward
Great-grandmother Jeffers' house. She had a
patch of cotton in her garden, and they must
have seen her chopping it.

They loved pine, as Thomas did, although they couldn't whittle it. Thomas' papa said the boys probably never would be as good at whittling as he was. Thomas had a talent for wood sculpture, so his father said. There were always folks coming from distances offering Thomas money for what he had carved. But Thomas kept most of his carvings for himself. He had a whole box of figures tied up in the trailer attached to the car. He intended placing them on counters and mantles all over the new house.

Thomas could sit in front of his brothers, carving an image out of pine, and they would jump and roll all around him. When the carving was finished, the twin for whom it was made would grab it and crawl off with it. Thomas never need say, and never once were the twins wrong in knowing what carving was for which boy.

They were fine brothers, Thomas knew.

If the new house is haunted, he thought, the twins will tell me!

chapter 2

THE SEDAN headed through the Pisgah National Forest in the Blue Ridge Mountains, and then out of North Carolina. Thomas had seen a sign and knew exactly when they entered Virginia.

"That's done with," he said to himself.

If Mr. Small noticed they had left their home state, he gave no hint. Mrs. Small slept or at least kept her eyes closed. The twins awoke, and Mr. Small told Thomas to give them their lunch. Soon the boys were subdued, staring out the windows and eating, looking far below at the bank upon bank of mist nestled in the deep valleys of the Blue Ridge.

Thomas was thinking about the new house in Ohio. The house was a relic with secret passages and rooms. In Civil War times it had

been one of the houses on the Underground
Railroad system, which was a resting and
hiding place for slaves fleeing through the
North to Canada. Such houses had been secretly called "stations."

When Thomas' father read about the station house for rent in Ohio, he had written
to the foundation that owned it for a full report. For years he had hoped to explore and
possibly live in a house on the Underground
Railroad. Now was his chance. But not until
he saw the report did he find out how important the Ohio station had been. Those
who ran the house in Ohio had an even
greater task than the care and concealment of
running slaves. They actually encouraged the
slaves to let themselves be caught and returned to slavery!

Thomas hadn't believed slaves went will-
ingly back into slavery until his father had
explained it to him.

"If you'll recall your history, Thomas, you'll
remember that the incredible history of the
Underground Railroad actually began in
Canada," his father had told him. Slaves who
had reached Canada in the very early 1800s
and established settlements there returned
by the thousands to this country in order to
free others. They came back for their families; they became secret "conductors" on
the Underground Railroad system. And they

returned to bondage hoping to free masses of slaves.

"But slaves continued to flee by whatever means," Mr. Small had said, "with or without help. Upon reaching the Railroad, they might hide in our house in Ohio, where they would rest for as little as a week. Some of them were given rather large sums of money and returned again to slavery."

"What would slaves need with money?" Thomas had wanted to know.

"Even a fleeing slave needs maneuvering money," his father had said. "He would need food and shelter and the best and safest way for him to get it was to buy it from freed Negroes."

"But the slaves connected with the house in Ohio were going back *into* slavery," Thomas had said.

"Yes," said Mr. Small. "And after they were caught and went back, they passed the hidden money on to other slaves, who would attempt to escape."

Still Thomas couldn't believe slaves could successfully hide money on themselves without having it found.

Some slaves did have their money found and taken away, his father said. It was dangerous work they were involved in. But others managed to return to bondage with the money still in their possession.

"Remember," his father had told him, "the slaves we're talking about weren't ordinary folks out for a peaceful stroll. Many had run for their lives for weeks from the Deep South. They had no idea how far they had to travel and they were armed with little more than the knowledge that moss grew only on the northern side of trees. Any who managed to get as far as Ohio and the Underground Railroad line had to be pretty brave and strong, and very clever. Most of them were young, with a wonderful, fierce desire to free themselves as well as others. It was the best of these who volunteered to return to slavery. They were hand-picked by Dies Drear himself, the abolitionist who built our house in Ohio. He alone conceived of the daring plan of returning numbers of slaves to the South with sizable amounts of money hidden on them."

"He must have been something!" Thomas had said.

"He was a New Englander," Mr. Small said, "so independent and eccentric, most Ohio abolitionists thought him crazy. He came from an enormously wealthy family of shipbuilders, and yet his house in Ohio was fairly modest. To give you an idea how odd he was," said Mr. Small, "his house was overflowing with fine antiques, which he neither took any interest in nor sold for profit. All the furniture remained in great piles, with just enough space to get through from room to room, until the house was plundered and Drear was killed.

"But when his plan to send slaves back to slavery worked," said Mr. Small, "there grew among freemen and slaves an enormous respect for him. You know, they never called him by his name, partly because they feared he might be caught, but also because they were in awe of him. They called him Selah. Selah, which is no more than a musical direction to raise the voice. And yet, Selah he was. *Selah*, a desperate, running slave might sigh, and the name—the man—gave him the strength to go on."

Selah. Freedom.

Thomas sat so quietly in the car with his eyes closed, he appeared to be sleeping. But his mind was full of thoughts about what else his father had told him was in the report from the Ohio foundation. The report went on to say that three slaves whom Dies Drear had hidden for a time were caught in an attempt to reach Canada. In truth, they were headed south again, but because they were captured on the northern side of the Ohio River they were believed to be fleeing to Canada. Their hidden money was discovered. Two of the slaves were killed by the bounty

hunters who caught them. That same week,
Dies Drear was murdered.

There had been pages and pages of the
report from the foundation. Thomas recalled
his father poring over it until very late at
night, often jumping up and stalking about
the room with obvious excitement. Then his
father had made a trip to Ohio. He was gone
three weeks, nearly ten days longer than he
had intended. While he was gone, Thomas
found the report and read it.

Thomas smiled to himself, his eyes still
closed. He had discovered something in the
report that his father hadn't mentioned.
There was a legend that came with the house
of Dies Drear. The report made light of the
legend, but when Thomas read it he was at
once frightened and pleased. The legend was
that two slave ghosts and the ghost of Dies
Drear haunted the house to this very day.

Right away Thomas had made up his
mind that the two ghosts had to be the two
slaves killed by bounty hunters. And the two
ghosts had then killed Drear in revenge for
their own deaths. But if all this were true,
Thomas was faced with a problem.

Why would two slave ghosts haunt a house
owned by the man they had murdered, who
himself haunted the very same house?

Deep down, Thomas didn't believe in
ghosts. But when night fell, when he was

alone in the dark, he feared he might see one. And if there were haunts in the new house, he wanted to be sure he had everything straight in his mind about them.

That way they won't ever scare me, he thought, sitting in the car. That way I'll know how not to get in their way.

When Mr. Small returned from his trip to Ohio, he wouldn't talk to Thomas about the house.

"Is the house really haunted?" Thomas had asked. "Did you hear the noises and see the flashing lights?"

"I thought I told you to stay out of my study!" his father had fumed. "I didn't give you permission to read that report. Besides, there are no such things as haunts."

"But is it true no one has lived in the house for more than three months in the last hundred years?" Thomas had asked.

"It's true," his father had to admit. "The house hasn't been lived in for very long at any time."

"Well, if the house isn't haunted," Thomas said, "who or what was it caused people to run away? And why would two slave ghosts stay in that house with the ghost of the man they had murdered!"

Thomas' father had become furious. His voice had been quiet, but filled with rage. "People are so full of superstitition, they

aren't able to see the truth when it prac-
tically stares them in the face!" he had said.
"Quit talking about ghosts. Don't ask so
many fool questions. All old houses have
ghost legends, and they are all poppycock!"
He had retreated to his study, slamming the
door behind him.

Mr. Small made a second trip to Ohio,
still not sure if he would rent the house of
Dies Drear. This time he was gone five days.
When he returned, he had the lease in his
hand. He was in high spirits. He hoped some-
day to buy the house, he told Thomas and
Mrs. Small. At last he made them a full ac-
count of his trip, the house and all its history.

"No," whispered Thomas. No, his father
hadn't mentioned the legend.

Now why didn't he tell the legend to
Mama? he wondered. Or does she know
about it, and he didn't mention it in front
of me, hoping I'd forget about it?

Thomas stared out at the steady rain and
the mountains, which were no longer familiar. Again he smiled to himself. His father had to be hiding something.

There's something in the legend I've
missed, Thomas told himself. At least there's
something more to the story of the two
slaves killed by bounty hunters, and Dies
Drear's murder. Papa meant to hide it from
me by not letting me get at that report.

But I know I remember most of what there was in it. It must be that whatever Papa means to hide from me isn't written down. It's something you would have to put together from what *is* written down. When he got mad at me and slammed the door, I must have been close to finding out. I just didn't ask the right question.

"Papa," Thomas said. "Papa." He propped his brothers one against the other behind him as he once again leaned forward on the front seat. "Tell again about Mr. Pluto, Papa," he said.

Thomas was interrupted by Mrs. Small awaking and stretching. "Where are we now?" she asked.

"Getting closer," Mr. Small said. "Outside of Bluefield."

"You mean Bluefield, West Virginia?" Thomas asked. "How many more hours until we reach the Ohio River?"

"Just be patient," Mr. Small told him. "You'll see the Ohio River in about three hours if we don't stop too long."

In Bluefield they stopped twenty-five minutes for lunch. Once they were on their way again, Thomas leaned forward to talk to his father.

"We were going to talk about Mr. Pluto," he said.

"Now, Thomas, he's told you enough about him," said his mother.

Mrs. Small didn't like hearing about Mr. Pluto. No matter how often Thomas and his father kidded her, she really didn't like hearing about anything that had to do with the house of Dies Drear.

She won't like it, Thomas thought. She hasn't seen it, but she doesn't like it at all.

"I want to be sure I know what Mr. Pluto looks like before I run into him," Thomas said. He had tried making up a picture of Mr. Pluto from what his father had told him. But that was hard; never had Thomas heard about anyone quite like Pluto.

Thomas' shoulders jerked nervously; he cocked his head to one side as he did always when he was about to listen hard. "Please, Papa," he said, "tell about him."

Mr. Small sighed. "I might as well," he said. "We still have a long ride ahead of us."

Mr. Small started talking and Thomas listened, letting his long arms dangle over the front seat.

"As I've told you, he's the caretaker of the new house," Mr. Small said. "Pluto isn't his real name, but another name for Hades, the Lord of the Underworld. Well, Hades had cloven hooves."

"I know that," Thomas said.

"Mr. Pluto has been lame in one leg for as

long as anyone can remember," Mr. Small said. "I have no idea how old he is. Neither does the foundation, which hired him years ago. He's spry, although that isn't quite the right word to describe the way he gets around. He's a big man, with white hair and a beard. I believe he has the most piercing green eyes I've ever seen. With that beard and hair and those eyes, it's no wonder he's known as Pluto. Otherwise," Mr. Small added, "he's harmless enough, and takes fine care of the place."

"The dream!" shouted Thomas. "It was him!"

"Thomas, please!" said Mrs. Small, holding her ears.

The twins began yelling, too, and Thomas had to hold them for a moment before they calmed down.

"I had this dream," Thomas told his mother and father. "Mr. Pluto was in it, but I didn't know it was him until just now!"

"Pluto knows many of the secret recesses of the house," his father was saying to Mrs. Small. "He was kind enough to show them to me. I'm glad we're keeping him on as care-taker—Thomas, I want you to be nice to him, no funny business. He's an old man with quiet ways about him. You could even say he's a bit secretive and strange. He rides around in a two-wheeled buggy drawn by two horses, one bay and one roan. He has a black, too, that he switches off with the other two. He's lived all alone on that property for such a long time, I'm sure he wouldn't know what to do without it."

"Does he live in our new house?" Thomas asked.

"No," said Mr. Small. "No, he lives on the other side of the hill from us. You'll be surprised by his house and the way he lives." He was about to say more, but seemed to change his mind.

"I'll warn you though," he said. "Pluto walks as agile as a cat. He came upon me while I was in the cellar. I hadn't heard him or seen him coming, and I nearly jumped out of my skin."

"Does he really look like the devil?" Thomas asked.

"Oh, anyone can startle you in a house as old as that," said Mr. Small. "I don't think there's a straight angle in the whole place. All the ceilings are amazingly high. But Pluto's no devil. He did try to convince me not to live in that house. He was serious about it, too. He knows the legend, and I'm sure by now he believes it."

"Are there a lot of old people?" asked Thomas. "I mean in the town—old ones who remember everything and talk a lot, like Great-grandmother always did?"

Mr. Small was silent a moment. "You are going to miss her, aren't you?" he said.

"Yes," said Thomas, "I guess I will miss her."

"I'm sorry she wouldn't come with us," said Mr. Small, "but she has that right to end where she began. Anyway, it's time you learned about young people. You are already wise in the ways of the old."

"I like old people," said Thomas. "They never need to know what you are carving out of wood or even why. They just wait until it's done and then they say it's good."

Mr. Small had to laugh. "You don't like to be bothered, do you? You have to be free. Well, there was a freeman's community in the town even during slavery. Many slaves probably settled there. There are young people and there are old ones who remember things."

Thomas had a jumble of thoughts he couldn't quite make come clear, so he began to ask question after question about the town. They had driven a long way before he did catch hold of what he was after.

"Papa!" he said suddenly. Mrs. Small raised her head from her pillow and looked around at him.

"Papa," Thomas said, "whatever became of that third slave?"

Mr. Small stiffened over the steering

wheel. He looked straight ahead, gripping the wheel with both hands.

Thomas held his breath for a second, then blew a silent whistle through his teeth.

His father began speaking so gravely and in such a low voice, Thomas had to lean very close to hear. "When we get where we're going. . . . Now listen closely," his father said, "because I don't want to tell you again. You are to speak to no one about the foundation's report on the house of Dies Drear, do you understand? And nothing about the three slaves. Don't even think about it, and speak of it to no one!"

Thomas sat back with his brothers, watching the bleak West Virginia landscape through the rain that right-flanked them in dull, white sheets across the highway.

So the third slave is the question, Thomas thought. I have found that much out.

Thomas' eyes grew heavy with fatigue. His brothers played happily around him. As he fell asleep, his mind curled around one thought.

But what is it? What is the answer?

chapter 3

THOMAS did not wake in time to see the Ohio River. Mr. Small was glad he didn't, for through the gloom of mist and heavy rain, most of its expanse was hidden. What was visible looked much like a thick mud path, as the sedan crossed over it at Huntington.

Thomas lurched awake a long time after. The car went slowly; there was hardly any rain now. His mother spoke excitedly, and Thomas had to shake his head rapidly in order to understand what she was saying.

"Oh dear! My heavens!" Mrs. Small said. "Why it's huge!"

Mr. Small broke in eagerly, turning around to face Thomas. "You've waited a long time," he said. "Take a good look, son. There's our new house!"

Thomas looked carefully out of his window. He opened the car door for a few seconds to see better, but found the moist air too warm and soft. The feel of it was not nice at all, and he quickly closed the door. He could see well enough out of the window, and what he saw made everything inside him grow quiet for the first time in weeks. It was more than he could have dreamed.

The house of Dies Drear loomed out of mist and murky sky, not only gray and formless, but huge and unnatural. It seemed to crouch on the side of a hill high above the highway. And it had a dark, isolated look about it that set it at odds with all that was living.

A chill passed over Thomas. He sighed with satisfaction. The house of Dies Drear was a haunted place, of that he was certain.

"Well," Mr. Small said, "what do you think of it, Thomas?"

"It must be the biggest house anyone ever built," Thomas said at last. "And to think—it's our new house! Papa, let's get closer, let's go inside!"

Smiling, Mr. Small kept the car on the highway that now curved up closer toward the house. In a short time they were quite near.

At the base of the hill on which the house sat, a stream ran parallel to the highway. It was muddy and swollen by rain; between it and the hill lay a reach of fertile land, lushly tangled with mullein weed and gold wildflower. The hill itself was rocky and mostly bare, although a thaw had come to the rest of the land and countryside. At the very top of the hill Thomas noticed a grove of trees, which looked like either pine or spruce.

The house of Dies Drear sat on an outcropping, much like a ledge, on the side of the hill. The face of the ledge was rock, from which gushed mineral springs. And these came together at the fertile land, making a narrow groove through it before emptying into the stream. Running down the face of the ledge, the springs coated the rock in their path with red and yellow rust.

Thomas stared so long at the ledge and springs, his eyes began to play tricks on him. It seemed as if the rust moved along with the spring waters.

"It's bleeding," he said softly. "It looks just like somebody cut the house open underneath and let its blood run out! That's a nice hill though," he added. He looked at the clumps of skinny trees at each side of the house. Their branches were bare and twisted by wind.

Thomas cleared his throat. "I bet you can see a lot from the top of that hill." He felt he ought to say this. The hill was hardly anything compared to the mountains at home. Otherwise the land in every direction was mostly flat.

"You can see the college from the top of the hill," Mr. Small said. "And you can see the town. It's quite a view. On a clear day those springs and colored rock make the hill and house look like a fairyland."

"All those springs!" Thomas said. He shook his head. "Where do they come from? I've never seen anything like them."

"You'll get used to the look of the land," Mr. Small said. "This is limestone country, and always with limestone in this formation you'll find the water table percolating through rock into springs. There are caves, lakes and marshes all around us, all because of the rock formations and the way they fault."

Mrs. Small kept her eye on the house. It was her nature to concentrate on that which there was a chance of her changing.

"No, it's not," she said softly. "Oh, dear, no, it will never be pretty!"

"Everything is seeping with rain," Mr. Small said to her. "Just try to imagine those rocks, that stream and the springs on a bright, sunny day. Then it's really something to see."

Thomas could imagine how everything looked on a day such as his father described.

His eyes shone as he said, "It must look just about perfect!"

They drove nearer. Thomas could see that the house lay far back from the highway. There was a gravel road branching from the highway and leading to the house. A weathered covered bridge crossed the stream at the base of the hill. Mr. Small turned off the highway and stopped the car.

"There's been quite a rain," he said, "I'd better check the bridge."

Now Thomas sat with his hands folded tightly beneath his chin, with his elbows on his knees. He had a moment to look at the house of Dies Drear, the hill and the stream all at once. He stared long and hard. By the time his father returned, he had everything figured out.

They continued up the winding road, the house with its opaque, watching windows drawing ever nearer.

The stream is the moat. The covered planks over it are the drawbridge, Thomas thought. And the house of Dies Drear is the castle.

But who is the king of all this? Who will win the war?

There was a war and there was a king. Thomas was as sure of this as he was certain the house was haunted, for the hill and house were bitten and frozen. They were separated

from the rest of the land by something unkind.

"Oh dear," Mrs. Small was saying. "Oh
dear. Dear!"

Suddenly the twins were scrambling over
Thomas, wide awake and watching the house
get closer. By some unspoken agreement,
they set up a loud, pathetic wail at the same
time.

"Look!" Thomas whispered to them. "See,
over there is clear sky. All this mist will rise
and get blown away soon. Then you'll feel
better."

Sure enough, above the dark trees at the
top of the hill was deep, clear sky. Thomas
gently cradled the boys. "There are new
kinds of trees here," he told them. "There
will be nights with stars above trees like
you've never known!" The twins hushed, as
Thomas knew they would.

Up close the house seemed to Thomas
even more huge, if that were possible. There
were three floors. Above the top floor was a
mansard roof with dormer windows jutting
from its steep lower slopes. Eaves overhang-
ing the second story dripped moisture to the
ground in splattering beats. There was a
veranda surrounding the ground floor, with
pillars that rose to the eaves.

Thomas liked the house. But the chill he

had felt on seeing it from the highway was still with him. Now he knew why.

It's not the gray day, he thought. It's not mist and damp that sets it off. There are things beyond weather. The house has secrets!

Thomas admired the house for keeping them so long.

But I'm here now, he thought happily. It won't keep anything from me.

The twins refused to get out of the car, so Thomas had to carry one while his mother carried the other. They cried loudly as soon as they were set on the veranda.

"They don't like the eaves dripping so close," Mr. Small said. "Move them back, Thomas."

Thomas placed the boys close to the oak door and then joined Mrs. Small in front of the house. His father was already busy unloading the trailer. The heavy furniture and trunks had come by van a week earlier. Thomas guessed all of it would be piled high in the foyer.

"It's old," Mrs. Small remarked, looking up at the dormers of the house. "Maybe when the sun comes out. . . ." Her voice trailed off.

Thomas placed his arm through hers. "Mama, it must be the biggest house for

miles. And all the land! We can plant corn
. . . we can have horses! Mama, it will be our
own farm!"

"Oh, it's big," Mrs. Small said. "Big to
clean and big to keep an eye on. How will I
ever know where to find the boys?"

"I'll watch them," said Thomas. "Wait
until it's warm weather for sure. They'll be
with me all the time."

"Let's go inside now," Mr. Small said to
them. He had unloaded cartons beside the
twins on the veranda. "Thomas and I will
have to set up the beds the first thing."

"And I'll have to get the kitchen ready,"
said Mrs. Small, "and you'll have to drive
into town for food. Goodness, there's so
much to do, I won't have time to look
around." Then she smiled, as though re-
lieved.

Mr. Small went first, and Mrs. Small held
the door for the twins and Thomas. At once
the boys began to cry. Thomas watched
them, noticing that they avoided touching the
house, especially the oak door trimmed with
carved quatrefoils. Mrs. Small hadn't noticed, and Thomas said nothing. He scooped
up the boys and carried them inside.

When the heavy door closed behind them,
they were instantly within a place of twilight
and stillness.

Thomas couldn't recall having been in a

more shadowy place, nor had he ever felt
such a silence that seemed to wait. There was
no small entrance room, as Thomas had
imagined, but a long, wide hall. One part of
the hall was cut by stairs, which rose in a
curve to disappear in darkness somewhere
above. Beyond where Thomas' father stood,
there was a wide doorway leading to another
room. Thomas could make out cupboards
there. It was the kitchen and it seemed to be
very large. On either side of the hall were
closed doors, which he guessed led into sitting rooms.

"Papa," Thomas said. He was growing uneasy just standing there. Mrs. Small mo-
tioned him to be quiet.

"What is it?" she whispered to Thomas'
father. "What *is* it?"

Mr. Small softly cleared his throat. "Nothing," he said, "but I had expected the furniture from the van to be piled up in this hall."

The twins grew heavy in Thomas' arms.
He found that he was leaning against a table.
He had been for some time. "Here's some
of the furniture," he said.

Billy turned to see and caught his ghostly
reflection in a mirror by the table at the
same moment as did Thomas. Billy screamed
and cried. Thomas was so startled, he nearly
dropped the boys. Mr. Small quickly found a
light switch. Now they saw a grand, gilded

mirror, on either side of which were two familiar end tables.

"Why, that looks beautiful!" said Mrs. Small. "Those are my tables, but whose mirror is it?"

"That mirror was there the first time I saw the place," Mr. Small said. "If you like it, I guess we can keep it."

He opened one of the doors off the hall, paused, and then beckoned them to come. He switched on a light inside. They saw that their livingroom furniture had been cleverly arranged to fit a much larger room.

"Who did all this?" Mrs. Small said. "How did they know I'd want it like this—it's just beautiful!"

"I don't know for certain who did it," said Mr. Small, "but I suspect it was Pluto. He's the only one who would think to do it."

They looked at the room. The two oversized easy chairs which Thomas had known for so long were placed side by side with a mahogany lamp table between them. No longer were they catercornered on either side of the couch, familiar, as they had been at home. They sat like soldiers on their guard.

The couch was placed across the room from the chairs. And between two of the floor to ceiling windows stood Mrs. Small's kitchen worktable.

Thomas gave Buster to Mrs. Small to hold.

He went up to the worktable holding Billy, patting the boy, who still cried. The top of the table had been sanded smooth and rubbed with linseed oil. All the old nicks and gashes from all the meats his mother had prepared on it had been worked away. And placed at either end of the table were plants of ivy in the white china tureens his mother had never favored.

"Who would have dreamed my old table could look like that?" Mrs. Small said. "And I never would have thought to use those tureens that way."

"It makes a nice decoration," Mr. Small said. "The table and tureens belong to another time. Mr. Pluto saw that."

Thomas turned slowly around. At the far end of the room was a massive fireplace. Old Mr. Pluto hadn't thought to build a fire there. But on either side of the hearth he had arranged Billy's and Buster's little rocking chairs.

Mrs. Small laughed on seeing the chairs, and Mr. Small smiled.

"Look, boys, there're your chairs," said Mrs. Small. The boys looked and then turned to Thomas. Thomas was still wary, so the boys refused to sit just yet.

As soon as Thomas had entered the room, he understood what old Pluto had tried to do. He had arranged the furniture in a rigid progression, with the two long windows, not the open fireplace, as its focus. Thomas' eyes swept from the fireplace to the windows, then out into the gray day, on and on, until he could see no farther.

It's his warning, thought Thomas. He means for us to flee.

"I don't like it," Thomas said, "I don't like it at all. And who is this Mr. Pluto to work out the cuts in Mama's table? He's sure taken a lot on himself. He's got no business in our new house!"

"I would have placed that table in some corner of the kitchen," said Mrs. Small. "I don't know why I even bothered to bring it, it's so old. Thomas, I'm surprised at you."

"It was thoughtful of Mr. Pluto to put the house in order for us," said Mr. Small. "I certainly hadn't expected him to."

But Mr. Small would not meet Thomas' questioning gaze.

He doesn't like Mr. Pluto doing this any more than I do, Thomas thought. I know he doesn't. He just doesn't want to upset Mama.

"Come, let's take a look upstairs," Mr. Small said. "I would guess Mr. Pluto put the beds up. It will be interesting to see what rooms he chose."

"Papa, are you going to let him take over?" Thomas said. "How does he know what room I want?"

"We can change your room if you don't like it," said Mrs. Small. "But if Mr. Pluto took as much time with the bedrooms as he did with this room, they will do just fine."

Thomas was shocked. His mother and father were allowing a stranger, and a man who looked like the devil besides, to walk right in their house and fix it to suit himself. He wasn't even a relative. He wasn't anybody!

"I don't want to see any more right now," Thomas said glumly. "I think I'll go out and look at the rocks and springs."

He sat Billy down in his rocking chair. At once Billy began to cry, clinging to Thomas' leg. Buster, still cradled in his mother's arms, began to cry too.

"Well then," Mrs. Small said, "you go with Thomas. I don't know what's got into you."

"I think they're just tired out," said Mr. Small.

"Thomas, you keep an eye on them," Mrs. Small said. "I don't think you'll have much trouble if you sit them far back on the veranda."

Once outside, Thomas placed the boys on the dry veranda and squatted between them. He put an arm around each one until they hushed crying. After they had quieted, he stroked them gently.

"What do you suppose that old Pluto is up

to?" Thomas said in a low voice. "Fixing things and arranging things. Maybe he hopes to get Papa to like him a lot . . . then he can rule everything. Well, he didn't count on us, did he? He's the devil and he won't be king!"

"Now," he said to the boys. "Mama and Papa are upstairs. We're all alone here. Tell me what it was about this door that caused you not to touch that pretty design. Remember? We came in the house through this door, and there was something about it you didn't like."

The twins stayed quiet. Thomas knew they couldn't tell him anything. But he was used to questioning them and finding answers in himself.

Thomas got up to examine the front steps. They were weathered but recently painted white as was the rest of the house. He examined the oak door and saw nothing unusual. He bent close to study the quatrefoil designs that were carved on the doorframe. They were shaped like petals. He was ready to turn away, when he found something. One petal, on a line with the doorknob, had a tiny, wood button in its center. Thomas checked, but not one of the other petals had such a button. He wouldn't have found this one if he hadn't been looking hard for something.

"So that's it," he said, "but how in the world did you all know?"

He took each twin by the hand, and led them up to the button. They bobbed from side to side, whimpering as if something hurt them. Thomas released them and let them sit on the veranda facing the barren lawn.

Cautiously he waved his hand over the button. There was a stream of cold air coming from around it. He glanced at the twins. When they stood, the air just about hit them in the face.

"It was chilly and you didn't like it," he said to them.

Carefully, and with a hand that was shaking, Thomas pushed the button. He pulled, he jerked, but nothing at all happened.

The twins fell into tantrums unlike anything Thomas had ever seen. They kicked their legs and flailed their arms wildly. They jumped up high and sat down hard, at the same time screaming at the tops of their lungs.

"You'll hurt yourselves!" Thomas warned them. He didn't touch them. He feared he might make matters worse. So he just stood there, looking down at them with his eyes darting all around.

"Quiet, kids! You'll have Mama come get you!"

It seemed that was exactly what they wanted, for they kept up the screaming.

"So you saw something!" Thomas whispered. His eyes were wide. "Something scary? Something I didn't see and couldn't take care of?"

Thomas thought of ghosts. Suddenly he was afraid, not for himself but for the twins, who could see but not say.

"Not very nice ghosts," he said, "if they have to go around scaring babies."

Thomas picked the boys up, balancing one on each hip. "But why would ghosts come just because I pushed a button?" he wondered out loud. "Ghosts?" he asked them. They whimpered and nestled against him.

"No," Thomas decided. "Something else a little more real." He hadn't the time to think what that might be, for his mother came then to see what was causing the twins to scream.

"They're just hungry, I guess," Thomas told her. "They were sitting there and then they started to cry."

"They're tired, too," Mrs. Small said. She took them from Thomas. "Now don't be long," she told him. "I'll have supper ready early. Mr. Pluto filled the refrigerator with food!"

Thomas held the door for his mother. He

waited until she was in the kitchen with the twins before he closed the door hard.

Mr. Pluto, he thought. Always Mr. Pluto!

He stood on the veranda with his back to the oak door; he took in all there was to see— the grand pillars, eaves dripping wet onto the barren ground, and the circle of gray mist beyond the lawn.

When he looked carefully, Thomas was able to see through the mist. He could make out the downward slope of the hill, with its rocks and springs, and the fertile land lying along the stream. He thought he could see the bridge and the muddy roadbed that crossed over it. Somewhere beyond that lay the highway. He listened, but could hear no traffic. All was silent. The only movement was the stream, rapid and swollen with the long rain, and the springs rushing into it.

Thomas was satisfied that no one watched him. He turned around to face the oak door and pushed the button in the quatrefoil. Nothing happened. He looked left and right and, at last, craned his head to see behind him. At once he saw what must have caused the twins' tantrum. The front steps were poised about a foot off the ground and wide to the left of their proper place. Where the steps should have been was a black and jagged hole about three feet around.

Thomas stood as still as one of his wood

carvings. With his back pressed against the oak door, he faced the steps and waited for whatever it was—ghosts, demons—that would rise up from the hole to challenge him. Instead, the sudden shock came from the side of the house.

He fell to his knees instinctively to hide himself. Coming forth now was the queerest sight he'd seen in all his life.

chapter 4

OUT OF THE trees on the right side of the house came walking the blackest, biggest horse Thomas could remember seeing. Maybe it was not as huge as he thought at first, but he was closer to it than he had ever been to a horse. Riding on it was a tiny girl, sitting straight and tall. She had a white, frilly nightcap on her head and she wore red flannel pajamas with lace at the neck and sleeves. She had no shoes on her feet and she sat well forward, her toes clasped in the horse's mane. With her arms folded across her chest, she stared into the distance. She was serene and happy and seemed not to notice Thomas.

Following the horse was a big boy about Thomas' age. He was stronger and heavier than Thomas, and his arm muscles bulged as he pulled back on the horse's tail.

"Whoa, you black!" he said in a loud whisper. "You mean old devil! Let my Pesty off, you hear, before I break off your tailbone! Pesty, you get down off of him. Please? Come on, make him stop, I've got to get my supper before it's all gone!"

The little girl paid no attention to him. Once she laughed and then turned the horse with just her toes. She circled the lawn, with the big boy pulling hard on the horse's tail. The horse didn't seem to care. Soon they came toward the house again, right for the steps and Thomas.

Thomas felt for the wood button, but he couldn't find it unless he took his eyes off the little girl, the horse and the boy. They were very close, almost to the steps, and the boy was yelling for the girl to stop that horse.

"You want him to fall down under them steps? You going to walk him right through that door?"

But the child knew what she was doing. She gently nudged the horse; it stopped in front of the hole. She looked at Thomas as though she'd known he was there all the time, and smiled very sweetly at him.

Coming around the horse's flank, the boy bent delicately to look into the hole. He was aware of Thomas. Thomas could tell. Both children were playing a game with him, and he could not figure out the rules.

"Anybody go foolin' around down there maybe will get lost forever," the boy said. "Maybe get lost in one of Mr. Pluto's tunnels and never get found again."

"Nothing down there," said the child. "Nothing but sounds."

"Now how do you know that?" asked the boy. "I bet there's plenty down there nobody's run into yet."

"Mr. Pluto let me walk it," said the child, "and I know there is nothing."

"Pesty, how many times must I tell you not to get too close to Mr. Pluto? He's going to make you disappear one of these times, and then how will I ever get you home to supper?"

"I'll tell him to tie you up," said the child. "Leave you in one of those tunnels for the ghosts to play with."

"Do you intend to go down under there?" asked the boy. "You planning on finding out how quick you can get scared in the dark?"

A few seconds passed before Thomas realized the boy was speaking to him. The boy still wouldn't look at Thomas, but pretended to be concerned with the hole.

"Who *are* you?" asked Thomas, still afraid and not at all eager to move from the safety of the door. "Who *are* you!"

The boy looked up at the child on the horse in mock amazement, then he quickly turned a polite, smiling face on Thomas.

"Well, how you been! How you feeling?" he said.

Now anger began slowly to take the place of Thomas' fear.

Then the boy said, "We are Darrow's children. I mean, I'm Mr. Darrow's youngest son, and that girl there, she follows me around so my Mama lets her stay. I call this girl Pesty. My Daddy calls her Sarah, and Mama calls her Sooky. Mr. Pluto, he calls her Little Miss Bee, and I guess you can make up a name, too, it won't matter to her."

"You mean to say she lives with you," Thomas said, slowly, "and follows you around—you all call her different names, but she isn't your sister?"

"I just have brothers," said the boy. He looked carefully at the child on the horse. "Still, she's as close to a sister as I guess I'll ever get."

"But where did she come from?" asked Thomas. Still on his knees, he had crawled out as far as the steps now, close to the boy and close to the horse. He didn't realize he had moved.

The child kicked the boy in the chest playfully and laughed.

"She came in a new tin tub," said the boy.

"It was night, and I was sleeping. I was five and I don't remember it. But they say that Mama brought her in to show her off to Daddy. And the next day I saw her and I've been seeing her ever since."

Thomas wanted to ask more questions, but now the child was asking him a question.

"What you doing on Mr. Pluto's porch? He'll snatch you baldheaded if he finds you."

"He's liable to turn Pesty on you, too, and that's the worst thing could happen," said the boy.

"Mr. Pluto just works here," said Thomas angrily. "This is my father's house. We are going to live in it, and old Pluto is going to work for us."

The boy fell into a fit of laughter calculated to make Thomas even madder. He slithered on the wet ground and pounded his fists silently. Even Pesty was giggling softly into the horse's mane.

"I think you children just better get off my father's land," said Thomas. He stepped off the porch. "Part of the Underground Railroad must be under these steps. I've got work to do."

"There's no train tracks down there," said Pesty. "There never was none that I ever seen."

But Thomas was not stopping for them. The boy stood up, eyeing Thomas seriously

now. Pesty backed the horse off so Thomas
could kneel down by the hole.

"You fixing to go down under there? You
want some company?" asked the boy.

"You'd just better get out of here," said
Thomas, not looking at him. "I don't need
any of your help."

"Well, I reckon that's true as far as it
goes," said the boy. "But I suspect you'll be
needing me later."

"We'll come back after awhile to see how
you come out," said the child on the horse.
And then she and the boy fell into more
laughter.

"Naw," said the boy laughing. "Naw,
Pesty, you can't come back today. You are all
ready for bed in your pajamas, and after
supper I'm going to lock you up so you can't
bother this here new boy. How you like
Pesty's pretty night clothes, new boy? She
likes to wear red because Mr. Pluto told her
red was the best color. Mr. Pluto likes red because it is the color of fire, and he is the
keeper of fire. Pesty is the keeper's helper!"
The boy laughed and laughed.

Thomas was excited at having met such
odd children. But he hid his feelings from
them by turning calmly away. "You get out
of here," he said, "before I call my father!"

"Oh, we're going," said the boy. "And I'm
M. C. Darrow, the youngest."

"I don't really care who you are," said Thomas right back at him. "I am Thomas Small, the oldest son of my father."

"But you can just call me Mac," said M. C. Darrow. "Everybody calls me Mac, even Mr. Pluto, when I let him get close enough."

Thomas didn't say anything. Lying flat on his stomach, he looked into the hole; his head and shoulders disappeared inside. It was then he lost his grip and fell head first into thin, black air. He landed some five feet down, on damp sod that smelled like a mixture of yellow grass and mildew. All the breath was knocked out of him. He lay there unable to move or think for at least ten seconds, until air seeped back into his lungs. Otherwise he seemed not to have hurt himself. He could hear Pesty and M. C. Darrow going away. Mac was talking quietly to the child. Then Thomas couldn't hear them anymore.

There was gray light filtering down from the opening of the steps to where Thomas lay, and he could see that he was at the edge of a steep stairway cut out of rock. The stairs were wet; he could hear water dripping down on them from somewhere.

"I could have rolled down those steps," he whispered. Mac Darrow and Pesty must have known there was a drop down to where Thomas now lay. But they hadn't told him.

"They are not friends then," said Thomas softly. He cautioned himself to be more careful.

I was showing off, he thought. I hurried and I fell. That was just what they'd wanted.

"Move slowly. Think fast," Thomas whispered. "Keep in mind what's behind and look closely at what's in front."

Thomas always carried a pencil-thin flashlight, which he sometimes used for reading in the car. He sat up suddenly and pulled out the flashlight. It wasn't broken from the fall, and he flicked it on. He sat in a kind of circle enclosed by brick walls. In some places, the brick had crumbled into powder, which was slowly filling up the circle of sod.

That will take a long time, thought Thomas. He looked up at the underside of the veranda steps.

Thomas got to his feet and made his way down the rock stairway into darkness. At the foot of the stairs was a path with walls of dirt and rock on either side of it. The walls were so close, Thomas could touch them by extending his arms a few inches. Above his head was a low ceiling carved out of rock. Such cramped space made him uneasy. The foundation of the house had to be somewhere above the natural rock. The idea of the whole three-story house of Dies Drear pressing down on him caused him to stop a moment on the path. Since he had fallen, he hadn't had time to be afraid. He wasn't now, but he did begin to worry a little about where the path led. He thought of ghosts, and yet he did not seriously believe in them. "No," he told himself, "not with the flashlight. Not when I can turn back . . . when I can run."

And besides, he thought, I'm strong. I can take care of myself.

Thomas continued along the path, flickering his tiny beam of light this way and that. Pools of water stood in some places. He felt a coldness, like the stream of air that came from around the button on the oak doorframe. His shoes were soon soaked. His socks grew cold and wet, and he thought about taking them off. He could hear water running a long way off. He stopped again to listen, but he couldn't tell from what direction the sound came.

"It's just one of the springs," he said. His voice bounced off the walls strangely.

Better not speak. There could be tunnels leading off this one. You can't tell what might hear you in a place like this.

Thomas was scaring himself. He decided not to think again about other tunnels or ghosts. He did think for the first time of how he would get out of this tunnel. He had fallen five feet, and he wasn't sure he would

be able to climb back up the crumbling brick
walls. Still, the path he walked had to lead
somewhere. There had to be another way
out.

Thomas felt his feet begin to climb; the
path was slanting up. He walked slowly on
the slippery rock; then suddenly the path was
very wide. The walls were four feet away on
either side, and there were long stone slabs
against each wall. Thomas sat down on one
of the slabs. It was wet, but he didn't even
notice.

"Why these slabs?" he asked himself. "For
the slaves, hiding and running?"

He opened and closed a moist hand around
the flashlight. The light beam could not keep
back the dark. Thomas had a lonely feeling,
the kind of feeling running slaves must have
had.

And they dared not use light, he thought.
How long would they have to hide down
here? How could they stand it?

Thomas got up and went on. He placed
one foot carefully in front of the other on the
path, which had narrowed again. He heard
the faint sound of movement somewhere.
Maybe it was a voice he heard, he couldn't be
sure. He swirled the light around over the
damp walls, and fumbled it. The flashlight
slid out of his hand. For a long moment, he
caught and held it between his knees before

finally dropping it. He bent quickly to pick it up and stepped down on it. Then he accidentally kicked it with his heel, and it went rattling somewhere over the path. It hit the wall, but it had gone out before then. Now all was very dark.

"It's not far," Thomas said. "All I have to do is feel around."

He felt around with his hands over smooth, moist rock; his hands grew cold. He felt water, and it was icy, slimy. His hands trembled, they ached, feeling in the dark, but he could not find the flashlight.

"I couldn't have kicked it far because I wasn't moving." His voice bounced in a whisper off the walls. He tried crawling backward, hoping to hit the flashlight with his heels.

"It's got to be here . . . Papa?" Thomas stood, turning toward the way he had come, the way he had been crawling backward. He didn't at all like walking in the pitch blackness of the tunnel.

"I'll go on back," he said. "I'll just walk back as quick as I can. There'll be light coming from the veranda steps. I'll climb up that wall and then I'll be out of this. I'll get Papa and we'll do it together."

He went quickly now, with his hands extended to keep himself from hitting the close walls. But then something happened that caused him to stop in his tracks. He stood still, with his whole body tense and alert, the way he could be when he sensed a storm before there was any sign of it in the air or sky.

Thomas had the queerest notion that he was not alone. In front of him, between him and the steps of the veranda, something waited.

"Papa?" he said. He heard something.

The sound went, "Ahhh, ahhh, ahhh." It was not moaning, nor crying. It wasn't laughter, but something forlorn and lost and old.

Thomas backed away. "No," he said. "Oh please!"

"Ahhh, ahhh," something said. It was closer to him now. Thomas could hear no footsteps on the path. He could see nothing in the darkness.

He opened his mouth to yell, but his voice wouldn't come. Fear rose in him; he was cold, freezing, as though he had rolled in snow.

"Papa!" he managed to say. His voice was a whisper. "Papa, come get me . . . Papa!"

"Ahhhh." Whatever it was, was quite close now. Thomas still backed away from it, then he turned around, away from the direction of the veranda. He started running up the path, with his arms outstretched in front of him. He ran and ran, his eyes wide in the darkness. At any moment, the thing would grab him and smother his face. At any time, the thing would paralyze him with cold. It would take him away. It would tie him in one of the tunnels, and no one would ever find him.

"Don't let it touch me! Don't let it catch me!"

Thomas ran smack into a wall. His arms and hands hit first; then, his head and chest. The impact jarred him from head to foot. He thought his wrists were broken, but ever so slowly, painful feeling flowed back into his hands. The ache moved dully up to the sockets of his shoulders. He opened and closed his hands. They hurt so much, his eyes began to tear, but he didn't seem to have broken anything.

Thomas felt frantically along the wall. The wall was wood. He knew the feel of it right away. It was heavy wood, perhaps oak, and it was man made, man hewn. Thomas pounded on it, hurting himself more, causing his head to spin. He kept on, because he knew he was about to be taken from behind by something ghostly and cold.

"Help me! It's going to get me!" he called. "Help me!"

Thomas heard a high, clear scream on the other side of the wall. Next came the sound of feet scurrying, and then the wall slid silently up.

"Thomas Small!" his mother said. "What in heaven's name do you think you are doing inside that wall!"

chapter 5

        "I SEE you've found
yourself a secret passage," said Mr. Small. "I
hadn't thought you'd find that button by the
front door so soon."

Mr. Small, with Billy and Buster, was
seated at the kitchen table. They were finish-
ing supper. Mr. Small smiled at Thomas,
while the twins stared at him with solemn
eyes.

Mrs. Small stood directly in front of
Thomas and then stepped aside so that he
could take a few steps into the kitchen.
Thomas glanced behind him at the tunnel,
a gaping space carved out of the comfortable
kitchen. He saw nothing at all on the path.

He sat down beside his father. There was
the good smell of food hanging in the air.
The twins seemed full and content.

"You knew about that tunnel, Papa?" Thomas said. He felt discouraged, as though he'd been tricked.

"If anyone came unexpectedly to the front door," said Mr. Small, "the slaves could hide in the tunnel until whoever it was had gone. Or, if and when the callers began a search, the slaves could escape through the kitchen or by way of the veranda steps."

It's not any fun, Thomas thought. Not if he already knows about it.

"Thomas, you frightened me!" Mrs. Small said. She had recovered enough to take her eyes from the tunnel and sit down beside Thomas at the table.

"Goodness, yelling like that all of a sudden," she said, "I didn't know what it was." She jumped up, remembering Thomas hadn't eaten, and quickly fixed his plate. Then she seated herself as before.

"Yes, why were you calling for help, Thomas?" asked Mr. Small. "You really made your mama scream."

Thomas bent down to take off his shoes and socks. A pool of water stood dark and brackish on the linoleum. "There was something there," he said.

Mrs. Small looked at him hard. Without a word, she got up and disappeared down the long hall from the kitchen toward the front of the house. When she returned, she carried a pair of Mr. Small's socks and Thomas' old tennis shoes.

"This is all I could find," she said to Thomas. She fairly flung the shoes and socks into his lap. Then she cleaned up the pool of water.

"There was something on that path," Thomas said. "It was coming after me as sure as I'm sitting here."

"You shouldn't make up stories like that," his mother said, "not even as a joke."

"There was something there." His voice quivered slightly, and the sound of that was enough to tell Mr. Small that Thomas wasn't joking.

"Then what was it?" asked Mr. Small. He watched Thomas closely.

"I don't know," Thomas said. "I didn't see anything."

His father smiled. "It was probably no more than your fear of the dark and strange surroundings getting the best of you."

"I heard something though," Thomas said. "It went 'ahhh, ahhh' at me and it came closer and closer."

Mrs. Small sucked in her breath. She looked all around the kitchen, at the gaping hole and quickly away from it. The kitchen was large, with a single lamp of varicolored glass hanging from the ceiling on a heavy, black chain. Her shadow, along with

Thomas', loomed long and thin on a far wall.

"Thomas, don't make up things!" his father said sternly.

"I'm not, Papa!" There was a lump in Thomas' throat. He gripped the table and swallowed a few times. He had to find just the right words if ever his father was to believe him.

His hands rose in the air. They began to shape the air, to carve it, as though it were a pretty piece of pine. "It was like no other voice," he began. "It wasn't a high voice or a low voice, or even a man's voice. It didn't have anything bad in it or anything. I was just in its way, that's all. It had to get by me and it would have done anything to get around me along that path."

"I forbid you to go into that tunnel again!" whispered Mrs. Small. She was afraid now, and even Mr. Small stared at Thomas.

Mr. Small seemed to be thinking beyond what Thomas had told them. "You say you saw nothing?" he asked.

"I thought I heard somebody moving around," Thomas said, "but that could have been you all in here. Or maybe it was the kids, come back to scare me."

"Kids?" said Mr. Small.

"The Darrow children," Thomas said. "I mean that youngest Darrow boy and that little girl he calls Pesty, that lives with them although she doesn't really belong to them. She came riding around the house in her pajamas on this big horse, and M. C. Darrow was hanging on the horse's tail. He was trying to get the horse to stop, but it wouldn't. Only Pesty could stop that big horse, and she was so little, too."

"What in the world . . ." said his father.

"Thomas, if you don't stop it!" warned Mrs. Small.

"Mama, it's the truth!" said Thomas. "There were these children, I'm not making it up! I can't help it if this is the craziest place we've ever lived in!"

"All right now," said Mr. Small. "Start over and take it slowly. You say there were children here?"

"Yes, they came from around the house just after I found the button and moved the steps." Then Thomas told all about Pesty, the horse and Mac Darrow. He even managed to make his father and mother understand that the children had been playing with him, toying with him, as if he were the object of a game.

"They were not friends," Thomas said finally. "They let me fall under those steps."

"No, they weren't if they did let you fall," said his mother, "but maybe they didn't know about that drop down."

"No," said Mr. Small, "they probably knew, but I would guess they had no real intention of causing Thomas harm. It was their joke on the 'new boy.' It wasn't a very nice joke and it was a joke that might have not worked at all. They were playing with you, Thomas, to find out what you knew. They must have thought you knew more than they did. After all, you came from far away to live in a house that no child in his right mind in these parts would dare enter. I would think that by now you are pretty famous all over town."

"I see," said Thomas. "Because I dared go into 'Mr. Pluto's tunnel'!"

"Yes," his father said.

"It wasn't a human voice I heard," Thomas said. "It wasn't alive."

They all fell silent for a moment. Then Mr. Small asked, "And you're sure you heard nothing more than that sighing?"

"That's all," Thomas said. "It just kept coming at me, getting closer."

Mr. Small got up and stood at the tunnel opening. He went into the long hall after a few seconds and came back with a flashlight.

"I'll go with you," Thomas said.

"I'd rather you stayed here. I'll only be a minute," said his father.

Mr. Small was gone less than a minute. Thomas and his mother waited, staring into the tunnel opening, flooded with the light from the kitchen. A few feet beyond the opening, the kitchen light ended in a wall of blackness. They could see the light from Mr. Small's flashlight darting here and there along the ceiling of the tunnel until the path descended.

Mr. Small returned by way of the veranda steps. His white shirt was soiled from scaling the brick wall. As he came into the kitchen, muddying the floor as Thomas had, he was thoughtful, but not at all afraid.

He walked over to a high cabinet on the opposite wall from the tunnel. Beneath it, a small panel in the wall slid open at his touch. The panel had been invisible to the eye, but now revealed what seemed to be a jumble of miniature machinery. Mr. Small released a lever. The tunnel door slid silently down, and the patterned wallpaper of the kitchen showed no trace of what lay hidden behind it. Lastly, Mr. Small removed a mechanism of some kind from the panel and put it in his pocket.

"Did you see anything?" Thomas asked him. "Did you find my flashlight?"

"I didn't see anything," Mr. Small said, "and I didn't hear any sighing."

"Well that's a relief," said Mrs. Small. "Goodness, if you'd found somebody . . . I'm sure my nerves would just give way."

"Your flashlight must have fallen in a crack," said Mr. Small. "I couldn't find it. Oh, yes, I removed the control from the panel. Without it, a giant couldn't raise that tunnel door."

"But you said there wasn't anything in the tunnel," said Thomas.

"That's so, but I don't want you wandering around in there," his father said. "The walls and ceiling are dirt and rock. There hasn't been a cave-in that I know of in a century, yet I think it best we don't take chances. I also removed the gears that control the front steps."

All he had to do was tell me not to go into the tunnel, Thomas thought. Give me a good reason and I wouldn't go . . . he knows that's all he has to do. He saw something or he heard something, and he's not going to tell anybody!

The twins had sat calmly through the commotion of Thomas' coming through the wall and their father going back through it again. Now they scrambled down from their chairs and slapped the wall with their hands. When the wall didn't move, they kicked it. They were crestfallen when the wall wouldn't slide up, as it had for Thomas.

Thomas had to laugh at them. "See? It's just a wall," he told them. They shook their heads.

"It's just a wallpapered wall with a pretty design to look at."

"I'd better get them ready for bed," Mrs. Small said. "They'll make themselves sick trying to get through the wall the way you did.

"Why is it you have to do just like Thomas?" she asked, teasing them. "Are you going to get into everything, just like Thomas, and cause me trouble?"

The twins laughed. Mrs. Small swept them into her arms and carried them out of the room.

Thomas sat at the table. He didn't look around the kitchen. He still wasn't ready to see the inside of the house, for he hoped to get the outside fixed in his mind first. When he heard his mother upstairs with the boys, he ate quickly. He glanced at his father, who sat across from him filling his pipe.

"It's still light out," Thomas said.

Mr. Small paused with the pipe. Thomas hadn't needed to say anything more for his father to understand his wish.

"Maybe you'd better wait until tomorrow," Mr. Small said. He glanced out of the window. There was still no clear sign of dusk in the sky.

Thomas picked at his food. He would not look around at the kitchen. The twins were making a lot of noise upstairs.

"Do I get to have a big bedroom for myself?" asked Thomas.

Mr. Small nodded. "Your room looks over the front lawn," he said.

"Does it have a secret door?"

"We thought it best that you and the boys have good, solid rooms. Mr. Pluto chose rooms that I would have chosen," his father said. "Better not tamper with the walls until you see how the tunnels and passages fit together."

He could at least let me have a secret closet, Thomas thought.

Still, he was eager to see the room, to put his possessions in order.

He thought, If that Satan, Mr. Pluto, has made it stiff and cold, I won't sleep there until it's fixed the way I want it.

Thomas' anger at old Pluto flared up and cooled. His thoughts shifted to what his father had said a moment before about the secret tunnels and passages.

"Papa, how *do* the tunnels fit together?"

His father explained that they were all of a plan. "Eventually, they lead in the same direction, to the same place," he said.

"But what if an enemy of the slaves knew that?" Thomas said. "He could just wait at that place, because sooner or later he was bound to catch somebody."

"No, Dies Drear knew what he was doing," said Mr. Small. "Let the tunnels meander like a maze, with subpassages and dead ends. Have the same sign or symbol marking the main passages, a sign that only the slaves would understand. And let the slaves reach that one place where there would be people waiting to carry them quickly in many directions going farther north. No, it wasn't likely that at the time anyone knew for sure what was going on in this house."

"Papa," Thomas said. He gulped down his milk to show that he had eaten. "It's still light out. I just want to see how the house looks all the way around. I won't go far."

His father smiled and said, "What is it you're looking for and why are you in such a hurry?"

Thomas wanted to tell his father exactly how he felt, but how could he say it? He didn't want to pry.

Papa, I feel you are keeping something from me.

Could he say that?

Papa, I see on your face that you are worried. You didn't like it either, that Mr. Pluto arranged our house.

"I'm not looking for anything," Thomas said at last. "I just want to try to figure out which rooms have the passages, after I've seen the outside. Like now, I know this kitchen isn't right. I haven't looked at it good, but I can tell something's wrong.

"Please, Papa," he said. "When it gets dark, I'll come inside."

Mr. Small took a deep breath. "You have perhaps an hour," he said. "Darkness has a way of falling down on you around here. It doesn't give you time to wander home, as it will in the South."

Thomas sat still for a second. He had a quiet vision of home. Springtime would be everywhere, and black crows sat all day, thick and shiny, in the fresh furrows of the fields. Just as the last sun slid out of the foothills, when you couldn't tell the crows from the earth, the birds flew in a mass into the air. The tips of their feathers caught the last sun, Thomas remembered. Their wings were blue and silver sails, like pinwheels. Then, the crows grew quickly smaller. The light slipped off them; the sound of them slid out of the sky. And the coolness of dark flowed over the hills. Thomas would walk from the pines to home with the night coming like liquid behind him.

He left the kitchen without another word to his father. Outside, he felt ready to explore. But he was unsure of the night that could trap him, and he was sad that he would never again walk those hills of home.

chapter 6

THE gray-painted veranda closed in the house on all sides. As Thomas crossed it, back and forth, he felt it separate him and the house from everything beyond it. Many times he walked the veranda, looking for loose or trigger planks. He did find a few creaking boards. Stepping on them hard, pulling at them, jerking at them, he at last decided they concealed nothing.

Whoever old Pluto is, he thought, he sure takes good care of things.

Thomas made his way around the house. He took notice of every window, flower bed and what few bad pieces of siding there were. He missed nothing of what there was to see. There were fifteen windows on the first floor, and five of them were floor to ceiling. He counted six 5-foot window boxes loosely packed with fresh earth and seeded already.

What do you suppose he planted in them? Thomas wondered. He leaned over one of the boxes. He could see shoots of some kind, perhaps summer and autumn blooms, but he didn't know much about flowers. He tried smelling the soil.

It smells sweet, he thought. Why did he have to *do* everything!

Thomas would have liked planting the boxes himself, carefully seeding them in evening, when soil seemed most fresh. He would have planted them with hyacinth, maybe, and pale green fern.

He might've planted them with poison, that Mr. Pluto, Thomas thought. Just a good-smelling poison. When you leaned over a box to see what was growing, you would get a whiff of it and that would be the end of *you*!

"Then he could be king," Thomas said out loud. "That's what he thinks he's going to be."

There were five entrances to the house. There was the front entrance, with the oak door and the steps with the tunnel beneath. There was one on either side of the house and two in the rear. One rear door led to the kitchen. The other looked quite old, was boarded up, and had been replaced by the newer one. Thomas examined the rear of the house more carefully. He had the feeling that there was something odd about it.

He backed away from the house to get a clearer view. Behind him, the land rose to the top of the hill.

There were trees up there—big, ancient trees, dense and wet with rain.

Just trees, he thought. If I climb one, I can see how the house looks from the roof down.

Thomas worked his way up the hill. Closer to the trees, he saw that they were a variety he didn't know.

"Won't be able to climb those," he said eyeing the sharp needles. He looked behind him down the hill and was surprised to find he could see beyond the house to the stream below it. He saw that the house hadn't been built directly facing the stream, but at an angle to it.

It looks like it faces the stream when you're standing down there, he thought.

Thomas squatted down to study what lay before him. Then he stretched out on the damp ground with his head propped on his elbow. Slowly he grew calm and tired. After what had happened under the house, he was content to be where he was.

"The house doesn't look so scary from up here," he said. "It's not pretty though, but that flat roof makes it look more graceful."

Thomas stared a long time at the house

and landscape, thinking of nothing in particular. He must have dozed. When at last he started and sat up, his legs were stiff. He got up, and his arms and face were cool.

He felt strange all of a sudden. He looked around him. The trees held darkness; below him, lights were on in the house. It seemed as though night had risen from the earth.

Thomas was ready to start down the hill as fast as he could go, when something rooted him where he was. He must have been hearing the sound for some time.

He couldn't move now if he tried, for the sound was dreadful, there in the dark trees.

"Ahhh, ahhh. Ahhh, ahhh."

It came from behind Thomas. The night was still; he could hear the sound clearly. Moving ever so slowly, he turned toward the trees. He listened for a long time, and, standing there, he became hidden by night.

Thomas was afraid, but it wasn't the first time today he had been afraid.

It's my birthday, he thought.

Papa, don't turn out the lights. Please don't.

He slipped through the trees, so used to walking in woods he could calculate where the pine boughs would touch him and have his hands in position to push them away. He walked on his toes, with one foot in front of the other. Indian scouts had walked that way so they could be ready to run in an instant if they had to.

Thomas followed that steady sound. His eyes darted blindly. Soon he was over the crest of the hill and moving downward on the other side. He didn't look back. He knew that by now the trees and hill blotted out the lights of the house.

"Papa, just keep them on," he said to himself. "I don't need to see them."

"Ahhh, ahhh," the thing went.

Thomas was getting closer to it. It was louder; there was something else—a crackling, sighing sound running beneath the ahhhing. The new sound was like dry leaves breaking under foot.

A lot of leaves, Thomas thought. A lot of them breaking together, with a wind coming up to blow them away.

The trees grew thicker. Thomas used his shoulders to get through them. He had the feeling he was moving too fast, and he tried to slow himself down.

You won't see anything quicker if you hurry than if you don't. You can't see anything anyhow.

His heart beat hard. As long as he didn't allow himself to think what the ahhhing might be, he could keep moving. Holding his mind as blank as possible made him less

afraid. Finally he was able to slow himself
down, but by then he had made his mistake.

The springy, slippery bed of pine needles
Thomas had been walking on was no longer
beneath his feet. His shoes clomped loudly
before he could silence them.

"Boards!" he said. He was walking on
wood. He still couldn't see anything.

The wood moved. Thomas began to slide.
He was standing on a platform of some kind
and the thing was rising. With his body off-
balance, he had no chance to run.

Thomas slid to the ground in a crouch. He
could see light coming from below the platform. The ahhhing had grown loud, with
the crackling, sighing, under it, trying to
catch it.

Then there was no sound. The light from
the platform reflected an eerie red and
orange in the trees. There was the smell of
smoke. Thomas hugged the earth.

Ever so slowly, two doors in the platform
opened. Thomas saw two hands and bright
fire, which turned the trees a slippery gold.
Out of fire and out of the ground rose a huge
head, huge shoulders. Up and up the thing
rose, with a head full of hair that was red
and yellow with light. The hair hanging
mosslike from its jowls bristled and tumbled
gold and orange.

"Who's that? What's that!" called a harsh, loud voice.

The frightful head looked down. Thomas saw its angry face. The eyes of it caught the firelight and glinted emerald and wet. The eyes of it found Thomas holding on to the earth.

"What demon walks on Pluto's house!"

"Devvvvil!" Thomas cried out shrilly.

He was breaking through the trees.

Devil!

Branches whipped at him; needles stung him. He fell twice. Once he got turned around, heading toward the fiery light again. He tripped and somersaulted, barely missing a tree. But he picked himself up and ran again toward his own house, up and over the hill. He was sure that the devil waited for him somewhere in the trees ahead.

"I've got to run," he told himself. "It's the nightmare! It's just like the dream in the car!"

It seemed to him he was moving ever so slowly. "I've got to run and hit it hard!"

When he ran into it, he would hit it with his full force. That way, he would cause it to pause long enough so that he could get around it and away.

But the man or devil, that Pluto, whatever he was, had fooled Thomas. He had not

moved fast enough to get in front of Thomas.
He caught up with him from behind.

He caught Thomas in mid-stride. Thomas'
legs were still running when Pluto's arms
tightened around his chest and, with ease,
swung him into the air.

It happened so suddenly, Thomas had the
notion that time had stopped. His mind went
blank. Then it began to function almost re-
luctantly again, as did his struggle to free
himself. One endless thought clawed its way
into and out of his head: No old man who
was lame, who was like any old man anywhere, even if he weren't lame, could ever
catch him from behind. No, nor lift him off
the ground and hold onto him.

Devil! Devil!

"Let go! Let me go!" Thomas whispered.

The man, that Pluto, heard Thomas and
laughed. It was a mean laugh, like a snarl.

"You rounders," he said, "think you can
come scare me out of my wits! You want to
know? I have found it before you, and you
ought to see it!"

Something bright exploded inside Thomas.
He had no time to put away carefully and
remember what Pluto had said. Now he was
awake, when a moment ago he had felt inside
a dream. He lashed back with his elbows, in a
motion that was swift and unexpected. Pluto

let out a grunt, and his body sagged just enough for his arms to relax.

Thomas ran free.

That devil was coming also. Thomas could hear him, and he was not running, but striding swiftly through the trees.

Thomas was over the crest of the hill. Below him were lights in the new house. The house was sweet to see. Thomas laughed—it was no better than a cry—and he ran faster once he had cleared the trees.

Thomas burst open the kitchen door, tripped over the threshold and slid across the linoleum on his stomach. He hit the table; dishes crashed to the floor. He lay there, trying to breathe. Someone bounded down the stairs. It was his papa. He heard his mother calling, "What is it? What's happening?" Somewhere above, the twins let out a tired wail.

Mr. Small was shocked by the scene that greeted him. Thomas lay sprawled half under the kitchen table, with broken dishes around him. There was mud on his trousers and a lone, dirt skid mark across the linoleum. The kitchen-door lock had been pulled completely out of the molding and hung, useless, by one screw. Mr. Small couldn't think why he had locked the door in the first place, since he knew Thomas would be returning by way of it. But he had, and now he couldn't imagine what force had pulled out the lock.

Mr. Small kneeled beside Thomas. "Thomas. Son," he whispered. He didn't touch the boy, but absently picked away bits of splintered glass from Thomas' shirt.

Mrs. Small came in and kneeled down. "Who did this?" she said. "Is he bleeding? Thomas! Please get up!"

"Lock." Thomas managed to say. He tried to keep his voice from trembling.

"It's . . . he's coming . . . lock." He was too tired to bother with making sentences. All he wanted his mother to do was lock the back door so Pluto—that devil, whatever he was—wouldn't be able to get him.

There was the sound of heavy feet on the rear veranda. A loud knock on the door caused it to slowly swing open. And framed by night stood that massive, black and bearded man some souls called Pluto.

chapter 7

A MOVEMENT of cool air from the open door fanned springy curls tucked behind Mrs. Small's ears. She'd never seen old Pluto. Her hands clenched, as some instinct to defend her family made her stand boldly in front of him. When the loud knocking started, she had moved forward. She stood there, not menacing but watchful and strong.

Pluto stepped over the threshold in a direct but courteous manner. He had thick, white hair and a full white beard, just as Mr. Small had described. And he was tall, taller than any elderly man Mrs. Small had ever seen. His broad shoulders drooped forward with age, causing his huge head to seem as untamed as that of a white gerfalcon.

What Mr. Small hadn't done was put the

whole picture of Pluto together for Mrs.
Small—his beard and hair against the dark
brown skin of his face, out of which peered
glassy, green eyes. He was somehow larger
than dream or nightmare. She studied him
from head to foot and did not think about
him being lame. It was something other than
his fearful head that caused her face to
tighten. The way Mr. Pluto dressed seemed
out of place and out of season, although
there was no one thing that was wrong.

Too well ordered, Mrs. Small thought.
Yes! Just too well groomed for a country
man!

The idea came to her that maybe Mr.
Pluto had planned with great care some particular effect.

But why? She wondered. She carefully
wiped her damp palms on her apron and extended her hand to this stranger.

"You are Mr. Pluto." Her voice was uncertain. "I shouldn't stare . . . my, gracious, I
was staring at you. I'm awfully sorry!"

Mr. Pluto walked near and politely took
her hand. He wore heavy hide gloves; they
looked new, and he did not remove them.
He said nothing. He retreated to a place
just within the open door, where there was
least light.

"This is Thomas, my son," Mrs. Small said.
She turned slightly in Thomas' direction,

where he still lay half beneath the kitchen table. There was an awkward silence in which Mrs. Small tried not to notice the mess Thomas had made. For it was Thomas alone who had caused the dishes to crash down upon his head. Mrs. Small slowly freed herself from the shock of Mr. Pluto, and, in the silence of the kitchen, she understood clearly what must have befallen her son.

Quickly Mrs. Small spoke again. "And this is my husband. I believe you two already know one another." Looking at Pluto, her features tensed. Her eyes darkened, as though shadow passed over her vision.

"Pleased to meet you, Mrs. Small," Pluto said. He was boldly cordial. "I'm afraid I mistook your boy." He cleared his throat.

Thomas, still shivering, watched Mr. Pluto secretly from beneath his arm.

"There are strangers . . . every once in awhile . . ." Pluto said darkly. "They come out here and they mean no good. I chase 'em off. I thought your boy was one. . . ." He nodded at Thomas by way of apology. His eyes flicked toward Mr. Small and quickly away before they could make contact. He did this several times.

Now why is he shifty? Thomas wondered. And he's a speechmaker, but he doesn't seem to know his speech, or else he hasn't written all of it yet.

Thomas shot a glance at his father. He couldn't have been more surprised by the look on his face.

Mr. Small stood stock still, in a pose of deep concentration. His arms were rigid at his sides. He stared so hard at old Pluto, his whole face seemed caught in a terrible spasm.

Thomas whistled silently through his teeth. Secretly he looked at old Pluto to see if he had noticed. But Pluto was staring into some neutral space above the table, as if waiting agreeably for what was to come next. Thomas had another look at his father, only to find him his usual self. Whatever had caused him to become upset no longer showed in his expression, nor in the way he stood there.

Was I seeing things? Thomas asked himself.

"Nice to see you again," Mr. Small said. He picked up his pipe and walked around the table to shake hands with Mr. Pluto. "I want to thank you for taking care of things. You did well putting the rooms in order— saves me a lot of time and energy. You'll work yourself too hard though."

"Why, the big moving van came at the beginning of the week. I took my time," said Pluto. "I hope it's all right."

"Couldn't be better," said Mr. Small. "Everything is fine just the way you arranged it." He watched Pluto as though he had been struck, suddenly, by some new and strange idea of him. Again Pluto would not meet his eyes, but appeared to pull back from him as far as he could without moving physically.

Mr. Small took a step toward Pluto and shifted the conversation without warning.

"How's the black doing, and the bay?" he said matter-of-factly. "I remember you were working on their shoes."

The question startled Pluto; there was no place for him to back up to without going out the door. "Oh . . ." he stammered. Mr. Small took another step forward. "Yes . . . yes, sir!

"The bay is fine, just fine." Pluto was talking fast, and Mr. Small did not move. "But I had to hobble that black," Pluto said. "He's got the chill, but he won't stay still. He tries to run all night to get away from it. I had to hobble him, had to tie his feet to keep him from bursting his heart."

"Horses?" said Thomas. "Papa, horses?" He was on his feet, forgetting his fear of Pluto. He thought of Pesty and that Darrow boy, and the black horse they had with them.

"Mr. Pluto has three horses, son," said Mr. Small. "I told you he uses two at a time for the buggy he gets around in. At night, he keeps them in the cave on the other side of the hill from here. The black has simple fever, which is odd, isn't it, Mr. Pluto, in a

horse of such dark color? I thought simple
fever hit horses with lighter coats, such as the
whites and grays."

"Yes . . . well." Mr. Pluto thought for
awhile. He seemed to struggle with his
memory, and Thomas watched him. Indeed
they all watched him, as though he were not
just strange, someone they'd only heard of,
but a man beyond their knowledge.

"If it was just a heat problem," Mr. Pluto
began, "say heat like they have in India, it
wouldn't have hurt the black. It wasn't the
heat though, it was nervous shock."

"I had no idea nervousness could act on a
horse's heat centers," Mr. Small said. He had
taken another step forward, and Pluto became agitated.

"Not nervousness," Pluto said. He squeezed
his gloved hands together. "Nervous shock.
Nervous shock! By haunted things nothing
living should have the unhappiness to see!"

At once Thomas had a vision of night and
Mr. Pluto's black horse grazing the hillside.
A specter floated slowly nearer, until it was
beside the horse. The horse lifted his head,
standing there for a second before falling
with a thud to the ground.

"Papa, ghosts!" Thomas whispered. "He's
talking about ghosts!"

Mr. Small looked sternly at Thomas; after
that Thomas stayed quiet. Then Mr. Small

looked hard at Pluto. At that moment, Thomas saw the faintest trace of amusement on Pluto's face. His father didn't seem to notice it.

"You have a sick quarter horse on your hands," said Mr. Small. "This is a lonely stretch of country. I'm sure the town boys like fooling around along the stream. Thomas, didn't you tell us you met two children out here today? One of them was a little girl called Pesty. She was riding a black horse, Mr. Pluto, and I believe she left the impression the horse belonged to you."

They all stood still in the room, with the quiet slowly closing in on them. Mr. Small's meaning had been clear to Mrs. Small and clear to Thomas. But if he had meant to startle Mr. Pluto with his knowledge of an unhobbled, seemingly well horse, he had been mistaken.

When Pluto started speaking, he didn't even bother to lift his voice above that hostile silence; he seemed not to consider that Mr. Small had raised the possibility he might be lying. Now he kept his eyes on Mr. Small's feet moving steadily forward.

"That Pesty!" Mr. Pluto said, fondly it seemed to Thomas. "She can do more with a wild animal than any small child should be able to do with anything!"

"You mean to say a child could unhobble a

full-grown quarter horse suffering from simple fever?" Mr. Small's voice was angry now.

"No," said Mr. Pluto quietly. "No, I mean to say that Pesty can ride that black anytime. Anytime at all, as long as it's day. But once night hits, that horse has the fever of nervous shock. And I have to hobble him so he won't burst his heart with running."

"You're not talking sense, man!" said Mr. Small. He was well on Pluto now and with a few more steps, he would be able to see whatever it was he was obviously looking for.

"Sense!" The word hissed around them, stopping Mr. Small's forward movement. There was a twisted smile on Pluto's face. Thomas still couldn't see that face as well as he had when the firelight had played on it.

"Sense," Pluto said again, less in anger than with sadness.

He looked gently at Mrs. Small. He looked at Mr. Small with that odd trace of amusement on his face. He stared vacantly at Thomas, then up at the ceiling. And he spoke in a kind of chant that sounded old and worn, like history.

"When hoot owl screeching, westward
    flies,
Gauge the sun ...
Look to Dies,
And Run."

Mr. Small stepped forward. Pluto moved into the frame of the gaping door. Like fluid, the tall figure of him flowed out and was the same as darkness. Thomas didn't even hear his feet on the veranda. But he was gone, leaving them free for awhile of whatever it was had possessed them.

chapter 8

"IT WILL just have to
hold until morning. I can get into town then
and buy a new lock . . . maybe two or three
locks, the way things look here. India! Can
you beat it? That's the puzzle!"

Mr. Small was speaking to himself. He
wasn't aware that Mrs. Small and Thomas
listened to him, so intent was he on his work
at the kitchen door. He had been working
on the door for the past ten minutes. He had
looked out once, right after Mr. Pluto had
disappeared into darkness, and then had
spent a few minutes trying to slam the door
shut. But without the spring lock, the door
wouldn't stay closed. He had taken two dinner knives and slid them in the groove of the
doorframe. One knife he placed by the lock

and the other just below the doorknob. He then slid the latch in place.

"No. No," Mr. Small muttered to himself. "Something else. Something different. Was it about the head? No, that was all right . . . perhaps the neck. The shoulders? If I could have just realized the difference when I shook his hand! If I could put my finger on it . . . *that's* what it was. The gloves! He's trying to conceal his hands. He might have burned himself badly. I've told him the kind of work he does is too hard for a man his age. And being the superstitious man he is, he will be afraid to see a doctor. He will suffer with pain as best he knows how, because a doctor has supernatural power the same as a ghost!"

Thomas and Mrs. Small listened. They understood that something had to be haunting Mr. Pluto. Whatever it was, part of it had taken hold of Mr. Small. Although he was finished with the door, he still stood before it, talking to it as if it were alive.

"Good Lord!" he was saying, "the man is history! He doesn't have to leave this land, that other side of the hill. And yet he is running just as hard as the slaves had to run, as if he were one! He stays here, colliding with the past on the one hand and the present on the other. But does he mean to run to the one and away from the other? Or run to both

and pull them together? Here he stays . . .
now why! Why does he stay?"

Finally Mr. Small sat down glumly at the
kitchen table, with one hand cupped over his
mouth. Thomas, after taking in the large,
lopsided kitchen, sat down beside him.

Mrs. Small busied herself by cleaning off
the table and sweeping up all the broken
dishes. She didn't utter a word to Thomas or
his father. When she had finished, she depos-
ited all the trash in an empty carton as
quietly as she could.

"I think I could do with more coffee," Mr.
Small said finally. His voice no longer held
that feverish, crazy sound, Thomas noticed.

If he goes around talking to some more
doors, Thomas thought, I'm just going to
have Mama take him to a hospital.

"It's still good and hot," Mrs. Small said.
"Thomas, will you have your coffee black,
too?"

Thomas was so surprised he couldn't think
of anything to say. His mother never allowed
him black coffee. What small amount of
coffee she would permit him to have came
only at Christmas or Thanksgiving, and then
it was mostly cream and sugar with a dash of
cinnamon.

"Oh, I know," Mrs. Small said to him, "but
you know you'd dearly love to have it strong
and black, the way your papa does. And since

you're sitting here . . . well, it's your birthday."

She poured two full cups of black coffee, placing one cup in front of Thomas and one in front of Mr. Small. She then poured a half cup for herself and sat down between them.

The smell of coffee filled the room. It flooded Thomas' mind with kitchen and coffee memories of long ago.

Mr. Small raised his cup. "Happy birthday, Thomas," he said quietly.

"Yes," Mrs. Small said, "happy birthday!"

So it was that Thomas had his first full cup of bittersweet, black, black coffee. He felt so good sitting there in the new kitchen, in the new house, with his mother and father. He felt as though he were at the center of whatever would happen next. Talk would happen next. He could tell that by his mother's excited face and his father's solemn one. They would talk things out the way they always had. Late at night, he'd often heard them in the kitchen talking things out, with that pure, hot smell of coffee filtering up to his room.

"Mama," Thomas said after awhile. He had taken a few sips of coffee. ". . . do you think now you are here and have seen everything that you'll ever want to go back home?"

Mrs. Small sat very still. Thomas thought she looked tired. He knew he was tired—all

of them were. But he had to know right now
how she felt about staying in the new house.
And he knew none of them wanted to think
about Mr. Pluto just yet.

"No, Thomas," said Mrs. Small, "I don't
think so. Your father and I have moved
around quite a bit, it's true. We travelled this
whole country in a camper we made ourselves."

"Looking . . . looking," Mr. Small said
quietly.

"We finally settled in North Carolina,"
said Mrs. Small, "and we stayed there a good
long while. But it was never right for us. No.
No, never go back."

"And you won't be afraid of Mr. Pluto?"
Thomas couldn't help asking.

"Thomas!" Mr. Small spoke sharply. "Nobody talking about ghosts and chanting verse
is going to scare us out of this house. Nobody
is going to take it away from us."

"Do you think he will try?" Thomas said.

His father was silent. He rubbed his jaw
thoughtfully, but said nothing.

"Well," said Mrs. Small, as though to
answer Thomas and clear their thinking at
the same time. She looked searchingly at Mr.
Small.

"Mr. Pluto *is* the strangest man, isn't he? I
mean, you never ever told me he was such a
huge man and such an odd-acting man."

"Well, he didn't seem . . ." began Mr. Small, "I mean to say, he wasn't at all . . ."

For the second time this night, Thomas watched his father become rigid, his face controlled by an instant spasm. Mr. Small rose swiftly from the table.

"We won't talk anymore about Pluto tonight," he said.

"But, Papa," Thomas protested, "we just got going on him."

"Tomorrow is Sunday, Thomas," Mr. Small said sternly.

Mrs. Small sucked in her breath. "Sunday," she said. "My goodness, how in the world did I forget! I don't have our clothes unpacked!" She looked worried. "I can't remember where I put my hatboxes!"

"Oh, for heaven's sakes," said Mr. Small. "There will be plenty of time for your hatbox search in the morning if we all get to bed now. Thomas, you go ahead. Your room is at the end of the hall, on the right side as you go down the hall. Get your pajamas out of the suitcase, and your towel, too. Don't forget your toothbrush."

"It's going to be Sunday all right," Thomas said. "We'll probably meet just everybody!"

"I don't doubt that," said Mr. Small.

"I did want to see the house tonight though," Thomas said. He looked around at the lopsided kitchen. "I can tell straight off this room is smaller than it should be."

"That's because you've had time to see the house from the outside," Mr. Small said.

"Let me see if I can figure it out," said Thomas.

"I want you to go to bed. Here," his father said, "I'll show you myself to save time."

On either side of the kitchen door there were sliding panels, which vanished into the wall at Mr. Small's touch. Within were arched cubicles, large enough for a man stooping to hide.

"Why, I wouldn't have imagined!" said Mrs. Small.

"That's great!" Thomas said. "Boy, I wouldn't have thought they were there either."

"A very temporary measure," Mr. Small said. "Slaves might be hidden in these walls for a short time, until the trapdoor could be raised so they could escape through the tunnel."

"Old Dies Drear thought of everything," said Thomas, clearly impressed.

"Now go upstairs," Mr. Small said. "The twins have the room across from yours, so be quiet. We'll be up shortly."

"Papa, you won't be able to get locks tomorrow," Thomas said, "because it's going to be Sunday."

"Maybe I can find out where a locksmith lives," Mr. Small answered. "I did forget for a minute that it would be Sunday. You go on up. Good night."

Thomas went up to his room, treading softly down the carpeted hallway. The hall was not well lighted, and the ceiling was very high. There were closed, varnished doors on either side. Tall and dark, they didn't seem at all friendly.

Why do I have to be so far away from the stairs? Thomas wondered. I'll never be able to hear a sound back here!

He stopped long enough to find out if he could hear his mother and father talking. The silence made him feel he was smothering.

"That proves it," he said. "You wouldn't be able to hear anything coming *or* going. You'd just be a sitting duck!"

He thought of looking in all the rooms before going into his own bedroom. And he did march up to one door about halfway down the hall. For some reason, he couldn't bring himself to turn the knob.

"Better wait until tomorrow," he told himself and backed away from the door.

At his own door, at the end of the hall, he held on tightly to the doorknob but didn't turn it. It was a brass knob. It felt cold. He looked across the hall, seeing the twins' room.

Their door was open, and a yellow nightlight shone through the darkness.

Gathering his courage, Thomas opened the door to his room and was at once blinded by bright light. There was a clear, glass globe suspended by a chain from the ceiling. The room was larger than he could have hoped, with a narrow fireplace to his left at the far end. There were two long windows across from him; his bed was placed between them, facing the door. There were smaller garret windows on each side of the fireplace. Directly in front of the fireplace was a large, old-fashioned captain's chair. It was a ghostly chair, with its back to the room; it faced the bare, charred insides of the cold hearth. Thomas had the awful notion that someone he couldn't see was sitting in it.

"Hello," he said. "Who do you think you are?"

He hoped to startle anyone who might be there into some sudden movement. He still held onto the doorknob, half in and half out of the room. He could yell and run fast down the hall if he had to.

There was no movement from the chair. There was no sound of any kind in the room except his own breathing. He came cautiously inside, leaving the door slightly ajar. Going up to the chair at an angle, he saw that it was empty. At the same moment, he noticed that he was cold and clammy.

"Whose old chair is it anyway?" he said out loud.

The chair wasn't one that had come from their home in North Carolina. Its cumbersome, hard seat and back were upholstered with faded leather. The flat, wood armrests were not even carved, and the base of it, made from the same hardwood, sat squarely on the floor.

"I've got to move it," Thomas told himself. "I'll never get to sleep if I don't turn it around."

As he struggled to move the heavy chair, he thought of fifty ways to get even with old Pluto for putting the chair with its back to the room.

He did it just to scare me. He's just a mean old man! Thomas thought.

But he couldn't move the chair no matter how hard he tried. He couldn't slide it on the gray, musty carpet and he could not tilt it and swivel it the way his mother did when she had to move furniture.

Mr. Pluto had arranged the room with the same plan in mind as he must have had when he'd arranged the front parlor. Thomas began to form a plan of his own as he went about getting ready for bed. He wasn't going to sleep in the room, that was for certain.

Not until I change everything. Not until I get that chair into some corner.

Thomas' old bookcase stood next to his bed, blocking the view from the lower half of the windows. On the other side of his bed, a crate of his books had been placed with great care. On top of that, his father had flung the smaller carton full of his carvings. There was a note attached to it as a reminder for him to put the contents away.

He took a few of his best carvings and grouped them at one end of the fireplace. That made things a little better, he thought. The view from the bed to the mantel of the fireplace was less balanced. Then Thomas opened his suitcase at the foot of the bed and got into his pajamas. He threw his clothes over the back of the chair. That made the room look almost messy. He smiled, relaxing a little. After that he lay down on his bed and stared up into the light.

The ceiling of the room was painted the dullest gray Thomas had ever seen. The color of it was worse than the carpet, which was dimmer still. The walls were papered in a pale blue flower pattern with loops of brownish leaves. Automatically, Thomas let his mind redo the walls and ceiling in bright earth colors.

Windowframes   and   baseboards   were

trimmed a dark mahogany. The floor where the carpet ended was the same mahogany.

I'll let the floor stay dark, Thomas thought. But all the trim he allowed his mind to paint pure white.

There were two more mahogany doors in the wall across from him. Thomas leaped up from the bed and snatched one of them open.

"Only an old, empty closet," he said. "I knew it."

It was not a large closet; it had a few hangers spaced about two inches apart along one wood pole. Thomas hung his Sunday suit in the closet and left the closet door open.

Treading barefoot, he went to the next door and flung it open. There was a tiny room with a sink and a three-paneled mirror above it. Thomas was pleased, and he remembered to brush his teeth. He even washed his face, eyeing himself in the three mirrors. After that he gave one last look around the room, especially at the chair, and turned out the light.

Lying with his arms over his eyes, Thomas tried not to think about anything. He didn't want to scare himself about what he planned to do. Soon he heard a door open and close down the hall; then the voices of his mother and father. He'd wait about an hour and then he would take the sheets from the bed and carry them downstairs to the front parlor. He was going to sleep all night on the couch, where he could see anything coming up on the front porch and where he might hear something coming through the kitchen.

Thomas was tired, but he did stay awake. When he thought an hour had passed, he did as he had planned. He made a ball of his bedding and stealthily headed down the hall. Thank goodness there was a runner on the hall and stairs. His mother had helpfully left the dim hall light on.

Once downstairs, Thomas felt a lot better. He looked at himself in the ornate mirror just beyond the oak door, right next to the parlor. He couldn't see himself well, but he was sure he must look brave. He went right into the parlor.

Without any light save what night glow came through the windows, he made his bed on the sofa. He felt almost calm as he settled down. Quickly he lapsed into semisleep, before going off altogether. Once he thought he heard water running somewhere, but that was an ordinary sound and he didn't bother to wake himself. Vaguely, he heard the slightest movement, not far away. But he was too tired, too deeply gone. He had not even bothered to close the parlor door.

Thomas was sound asleep when suddenly

the upstairs hall light went off. Awhile after that, there was again the sound of running water. Then the hall mirror near the oak door swung silently open. And through it all Thomas slept.

Soundlessly the mirror closed. Whatever stood there in front of it gave back no reflection in the totally dark house. The thing was not the same as night. It was darkness detached from the black of the entranceway. It was solid, but it could move, and it did not hesitate. It went directly to the stairs and up them, a mass of shadow-black that knew its way. At the top of the stairs, it paused as though listening. All remained silent. The thing, as it stopped before each closed door, was once more a part of the black house.

It pressed itself against each doorjamb, on the right side, but did not try to enter any room. Near the twins' room, where the yellow light still glowed, it became more visible. Now it was massive, bold. Not vapor, not blackness, it was not ghostly at all. It was a thing become manlike.

It moved across to the twins' room, skirting the light, where it placed something dimly metallic in the doorframe. It crossed back to Thomas' room, doing the same. It did not move; it listened a long while. Then it crossed over to Mr. and Mrs. Small's room, where it again placed something in the doorframe. After that it went down the hall and down the stairs.

Whatever it was did not bother looking at Thomas asleep in the parlor. Perhaps it didn't know he was there. It vanished behind the mirror, the way it had come. All was still once more. The night passed, as dawn came creeping into the house through the parlor windows.

chapter 9

THOMAS was talking to himself in his sleep. He could hear himself; he could feel the shape of words in his mouth. He became half conscious and recognized the sounds of birds singing in the trees outside the house. They were so many and so loud, they were noisy. But sleep overcame him again. He dreamed of trees and the danger of Mr. Pluto.

Later he awoke with a start and sat up on the couch. Clear morning sunlight filled the parlor. Whatever he'd said in his sleep, he couldn't remember now.

Was it a dream? he wondered. I've forgotten something. Was it a dream I've forgotten?

Across the foot of the couch lay his new suit and fresh underwear. There was a note pinned to his shirt from his mother. Thomas read it and laughed. It said, "Thomas, you are to wear these clothes."

He recalled the day was Sunday and jumped up to get dressed.

"Anyhow," he said out loud, "I can't remember if it was a dream or not. I've got to think about what it is I've forgotten. But not today. No, not today!"

He hurried to the kitchen, still fumbling with his tie. The table was set; there were glasses filled with juice. But there was no one about, not even his mother. The oven was on. Thomas peeked inside.

"Good!" he said. "Good hoecakes just waiting. Mama must be missing Great-grand-mother. It's Sunday for sure!"

In sunlight, the kitchen looked much like any big kitchen anywhere. There were no shadowed angles to bring out its lopsidedness.

It looks almost friendly, Thomas thought. But I know there's the tunnel. I know about slaves hiding and running.

He went toward the staircase. There was not a sound from up above, although his mother had to be up, probably his father, too. The twins would be sleeping, or he would have heard them.

He paused at the mirror next to the front parlor and carefully surveyed himself.

My head is too big, he thought. But the suit is all right. Everybody will know it is a new suit. I will tell them I got it for my birthday.

He straightened his tie.

Maybe we'll bring some folks home with us. They will sit in the parlor with Papa. They won't like him at first because he's a teacher. But they'll come because they'll want to know why we are here and living in this house. They'll like him once they hear him talk.

It seemed to Thomas that his father talked best on Sunday. He always spoke of history—not only the history of black people, but American Indian history and the history of the Hebrew tribes. Once, when they had a minister back home, he would often stop by on Sunday to listen to Thomas' father and to have a cup of coffee. Thomas felt very proud at those times. But usually, there were just ordinary people in their house on Sunday.

Some neighbors. Or his two uncles and their families, who would come one Sunday a month for talk, all the way from Tennessee.

"There's no minister anymore," he whispered. "I said I wasn't going to think about home. I said I wouldn't."

Folks will come to visit here just like they did at home, he told himself. I'll have friends like I never had before, you wait and see.

At the top of the stairs, Thomas couldn't have been more startled by what he saw. His father sat in his best suit, cross-legged on the floor in the middle of the hallway. His mother kneeled beside him in her gray wool suit and her brand-new, white-and-black straw hat. They were completely silent, and Thomas' father was examining something he held in his palm.

Thomas tiptoed up to them and knelt down. "What have you got there?" he asked his father.

Mr. Small had three metallic objects spread out on his hand. He didn't answer Thomas; instead, he carefully placed the objects one by one on the floor.

"Triangles!" Thomas said.

"Three of them," said Mrs. Small softly, "and they're exactly alike."

"Yes, three right triangles," said Mr. Small, as though talking to himself. "Thomas, go to my room, fetch me my pen on the dresser and a sheet of paper from my briefcase. I have an idea we might be able to understand them better if we diagram them."

Thomas went and returned almost at once.

Mr. Small laid out the paper beside the triangles. Then he drew on the paper a large triangle that looked the same as those in front of him.

"The two legs of the triangle which make the right angle are wood," he said. "Probably a hardwood, like oak." He drew on the paper, marking each leg of the right angle with a capital W.

"The surface of the triangle, between the legs, must be tin. In any case, it's lightweight and coated with silver paint."

He drew a line to mark the hypotenuse—the side opposite the right angle. He then shaded the space between the hypotenuse and the angle and marked it with a capital S to show that it was painted silver.

"The angle seems to be real gold, I can't tell for sure." Mr. Small marked it with a G for gold, and seemed to be finished. "Wait," he said.

Next to the triangle he had drawn he wrote down each letter, and beside each letter he wrote an explanation of what the letter represented.

"Now let's see what we have," he said.

"You forgot something," Thomas said. He picked up one triangle to show his father. Hardly noticeable was a circle of metal in the wood, where the legs of the triangle joined. Thomas turned the triangle on its opposite side. Protruding was a metal peg about a half an inch long.

"Ah, you're pretty good, Thomas," said Mr. Small. "I'll show the peg with a black dot." He made the dot on the paper. The completed triangle looked like part of a puzzle:

W   legs of wood, forming right angle

G   90° angle of gold

S   area between right angle and hypotenuse: metal coated with silver paint

•   metal peg

Mr. Small began to arrange the three triangles on the floor to see if they fit together in any way. He thought of taking one and laying it over the diagram he had drawn.

Thomas picked up one of the other triangles and fitted it next to the one on the diagram, with the wood sides next to each other and the wood angles touching.

Then Mr. Small picked up the third triangle they had found. He fitted it next to the one Thomas had placed down, so that all three wood angles were touching.

"If it's a square, there's one missing," Mr. Small said. "The top one."

"Any one of them is missing," said Thomas. "I mean, you can move them so that there is always one missing, since they are three triangles just alike."

"It doesn't make any kind of sense," Mr. Small said. "Why did they leave just three triangles if they meant to make a square? Clearly, there's a triangle missing."

"Where did you get these three?" Thomas wanted to know.

"They were stuck in the doorframes on the outside of the three bedrooms we occupy," Mrs. Small said.

To Thomas, his mother's voice sounded breathless.

She's frightened, he thought. She's just scared to death.

"They weren't there last night. I would have seen them," Thomas said.

Then Thomas sat quite still. It struck him why his mother was so afraid. His eyes grew wide and searching.

"Yes," said Mr. Small, reading his thoughts. "Someone walked right in, not making a sound. While we slept, he, or they, came through our locked doors to place these triangles in the walls."

"A warning!" Thomas managed to say. "Mr. Pluto's second warning!"

"Warning? Mr. Pluto?" his mother said.

"The first warning was the way he arranged that parlor downstairs," Thomas said. "He made it so it was a progression going out the windows and on and on."

"You are letting your imagination get the best of you, Thomas," she said. "You don't know that it was Mr. Pluto who was here last night."

"It's a warning, I tell you!" Thomas said. "He means for us to flee. To flee south!"

All at once Mr. Small leaned very close to the paper on which he and Thomas had fitted together the three triangles. "Thomas!" he said. He began to move around the paper, looking at it from all sides. "It's an optical illusion. It's a box, true, but the wood legs form a cross . . . a Greek cross!"

"What in the world?" said Mrs. Small.

"Son, you are pretty good," said his father. "I don't know about that parlor, the way it was arranged, being a sign. That might be too much for a man like Mr. Pluto to think up. But this triangle is definitely a warning, and it could be a warning to flee. And now, all we need to do is wait."

"For Mr. Pluto," Thomas said.

Mr. Small spoke quietly. "We may not see anyone. But you can be sure there will be another triangle sometime, somewhere, and that we will find it."

"Papa, what is a Greek cross? You said the triangles made a Greek cross," Thomas said.

"I meant that we will have a Greek cross when we fit together all the triangles." He drew a Greek cross next to the diagram of the triangle and placed the three triangles on it. The top right triangle was missing.

He explained to them what a Greek cross was.

"It's also known as a St. George's cross," he told them, "the cross used on the flag of Great

The Greek Cross

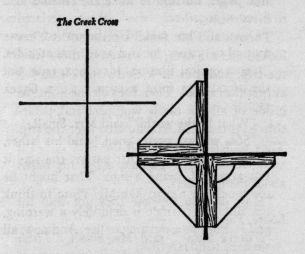

Britain. It differs from our familiar Christian cross, or cross of Calvary, in that if you connect the points you have four triangles exactly the same."

Mr. Small hesitated. "And why a Greek cross," he said, "where any one of the triangles can be moved to fit the place of any other?

"It's confusing," he added softly to himself. "If it's a warning, it surely says nothing to me at the moment."

"We'd better get the twins up," Mrs. Small said. "We're going to be late if we don't get out of here soon."

"I nearly forgot it was Sunday," Mr. Small said.

Mrs. Small hurried to wake the twins and to dress them.

Thomas and Mr. Small went outside. They looked the car over; it was quite dirty from the trip, and they took cloths and cleaned it as best they could. Then they cleaned out the inside of all the candy wrappers and potato chip bags that had accumulated over the trip. They pulled the trailer off the road onto the lawn. It was then Thomas asked his father about the intruders.

"How do you suppose they got into the house, Papa?"

"I don't know," said Mr. Small. "There are corridors I assume I don't know about. We'll have to take care." He looked cautiously at his son. "You had no business wandering around the house in the dead of night. You could have run into someone. Why did you move down into that parlor?"

"Well, because . . ." answered Thomas. He remembered the captain's chair facing the fireplace in his room. He couldn't let his father know he had been afraid of an empty chair. "Because I thought I would be able to hear somebody if they came in the front or back doors."

"Anybody stealing into a house in the dead of night isn't going to use the main entrances," said Mr. Small.

"I suppose not," said Thomas. He felt foolish. "I guess I didn't think."

Mr. Small drew Thomas aside, as though the lawn, the very trees, pressed close to the house might hear. "Can I confide in you, son?" he asked. "May I trust you with something and have you stay silent about it? I won't want to worry your mother."

A chill ran down Thomas' back. He was surprised by the seriousness of his father's tone. "Yes! Sure, Papa—what is it we've gotten ourselves into!"

"Trust me with that," said Mr. Small. "It may not be anything at all. And then again, it might be. I don't know for sure what's at stake. I really don't want to involve the police...."

"The police!" Thomas broke in on him. He fairly shouted, and Mr. Small had to tell him to keep quiet.

"We'll have to set up a watch," Mr. Small said. "Probably from midnight until dawn, until about five o'clock. You'll take two hours and I'll have three."

"I can take three, Papa," said Thomas. "I'm strong, I can stay awake."

"I hope we won't have to do it," his father said. "If things continue to happen as fast as they have been, there may not be any need for a watch."

"Papa, do you think that in the next day or two . . ." Thomas couldn't finish the thought. He couldn't get beyond the idea of having to call the police. Who was Mr. Pluto anyway, and what did he have to do with those funny triangles?

"Before this day is over, I think we'll know a lot more than we know now," said Mr. Small. "And if we do have to set up a watch, you'll patrol the upstairs. No matter what happens, no matter what you hear or see, you're not to leave that upstairs hall. Just give out a whoop and I'll come running."

"Yes, sir," Thomas said. "I'll yell like the devil!"

Somewhere there was the sound of horses' hooves. There was a whinnying nearby.

Mr. Small went quickly across the lawn to where the springs rushed down to the stream. Thomas followed close behind.

Thomas looked down on the stream and the springs running over the rocks. The stream sparkled in the morning sun, and the rocks were gold and rust where the water ran over them.

"Oh, that's about the prettiest sight I've seen," Thomas said.

"Look there," said Mr. Small. "You can see the spires of the college."

"You'll be teaching there," Thomas said, "and I can come on my bike every day."

"Would you do that?" asked Mr. Small. "We could have lunch together with the students in the dining hall." He looked fondly at Thomas. "That is, until you have so many friends you won't have time to take lunch with your father." He watched Thomas closely, for he knew his son would be most unsure of himself when it came to making new friends.

"Maybe I'll bring a friend or two along," said Thomas. "Maybe not every day because there'll be so much to do. But we'll come once a week for sure."

"I'll look forward to that," Mr. Small said. Bursting from around a bend in the stream came a buggy drawn by two horses.

"Papa, look! It's the black—the black that was here yesterday!" There was a lighter horse hitched up with the black. It was the bay Mr. Small had mentioned before. "And Papa, Mr. Pluto's driving. And there's that child with him, that Pesty I told you about!"

The driver was indeed Mr. Pluto. He had a black cape draped over his shoulders. It was held with an enormous safety pin across his chest. The cape was old and misshapen; it appeared he had made it himself, out of material such as monk's cloth. Although it was clean, it looked the worse for wear. He wore on his head a stovepipe hat, which tipped crazily back and forth as the buggy bounced along.

Pluto drove with one hand, holding the reins wrapped around his palm. He held a black and shiny whip in the same hand. The lash dangled from the whip in a curious, sideways S. In the crook of his free arm leaned the child called Pesty. She was dressed in pink tulle and a blue, polka-dot bonnet. Below pink silk stockings she wore white, high-button shoes. They were the queerest shoes Thomas had ever seen.

"Where are his gloves?" whispered Mr. Small. "I thought surely he had burned himself . . . but look at the child. A bonnet no less! And high-button shoes. That stovepipe is a knockout. History, I tell you, living history! Out of time!"

"Papa, he sees us," said Thomas. "He's slowing."

At the sight of Mr. Small and Thomas, Pluto brought the buggy nearly to a stop.

"Good morning to you," he shouted smiling broadly. "The bad weather has made its getaway, and I'm feeling good." He laughed loudly. "I see you all be going to Sunday, all dressed up."

"Good morning to you," Mr. Small said. He

was somewhat taken aback by the friendliness of this odd-acting stranger of the night before. But quickly he fell into the spirit of Pluto's good humor. "We are going to Sunday for sure—all of us, even my two little boys."

"That so?" said Mr. Pluto. "It's a long spell for the little ones. Preacher likes the sound of his own voice." He laughed again.

"Well, they will endure it," said Mr. Small.

"I reckon we all will," Mr. Pluto said. "Glad to see you folks are fine," he added. "Did you have a good night—sleep well there in the big house?"

There was a pause in which Mr. Small studied Pluto without blinking. If the old man had meant anything sinister by the remark, there was no trace of it in his eyes.

"We slept fine," said Mr. Small. "Couldn't have been better."

"Well, we'll see you there," said Mr. Pluto. "Glad you folks arrived and are feeling good."

He had moved off with the buggy when the child Pesty piped up. "Mr. Thomas," she called, "how you like my pretty new shoes?"

Thomas didn't know quite what to say. "They are nice, Miss Pesty . . . where did you get them?" he did manage to call back.

Mr. Pluto gave a whip to the bay. The

buggy leaped forward, drowning out Pesty's
tiny voice. But Thomas saw the shape of
what she spoke.

"Mr. Pluto got them for me . . ." The last
was something Thomas couldn't make out.

At the foot of the bridge, Mr. Pluto turned
his buggy into the stream. On the opposite
bank, he took with ease the incline to the
gravel road and disappeared down toward
the highway.

"If they aren't a pair!" said Mr. Small. "I
bet they dress up like that every Sunday, just
to get the goat of Sunday folks, the ones who
believe Pluto is at least part devil. But what
did he mean by the other, that's a puzzle
too."

"By the other what?" Thomas wanted to
know. Mr. Small had spoken almost to himself. Now he turned on Thomas a brooding
look.

"Why, the part about being glad we folks
arrived," said Mr. Small.

"I thought it sounded funny when he said
it," Thomas said. "Maybe he was just apolo-
gizing for being so scared of the dark and
ghosts and everything."

"Maybe," Mr. Small said. "Perhaps he was
ashamed of himself for mistaking you for
someone else in the dark. By the way, we
never did find out why you were running
in the first place. What happened out there

123

to cause you to break open the door and upset Mama's dishes?"

Thomas felt ashamed. All around them
was peace and quiet. Even the house did not
look ugly in the clear sunlight. There was
nothing at all to be afraid of now.

"It was spooky on top of the hill last
night," he said. "I went up there to see the
house from above. I was just going to come
back, when it got dark and I heard that
ahhhing sound. Papa, it had a funny sighing that went right along with it. I just had
to follow that sound and I was going fast
because I was kind of scared. I got going too
fast and I was standing on this big wood platform or something before I knew it."

"Oh, I see," said Mr. Small. "So that's
what happened."

"Then the platform started to move,"
Thomas said. "I slid on it. Next there was
fire coming up from under it, and Mr. Pluto
yelling at me . . ."

Mr. Small threw back his head and
laughed. "The ahhhing sound, you say, led
you to the platform?"

"I guess it did," said Thomas. "It had to be
coming from there . . . what's so funny?"

"And it was the same sound you heard in
the tunnel under the steps?"

"Yes, the same sound," Thomas said. He
looked doubtfully at his father.

"Thomas, I should have told you about that place before now, but I suspected you would enjoy discovering it for yourself. I never thought you would find it at night. You see," said Mr. Small, "that platform is one of the two openings in the cave in which Mr. Pluto lives."

"He lives in a real cave?" Thomas said.

"It's dry and clean," said Mr. Small. "It's as good a house as any above ground. It might even be better, because it stays fairly dry. I haven't seen it, but I've heard a good deal about it.

"Mr. Pluto is a blacksmith, son," continued Mr. Small. "At least, that's what he did for a living a long time ago, when there were enough horses in these parts to make his line of work worth doing. That ahhhing sound you heard along with the sighing couldn't have been anything more than his bellows working. I didn't hear it when I went to see if there was anyone in that tunnel under the steps. I suppose that's why I didn't guess before now what that sound was. Pluto must have heard you walking on the roof of his house. . . . Tell me, did you hear that sighing once the doors in the platform had opened?"

"I don't believe I heard it after that," Thomas said.

"That's it then," said Mr. Small. "When

Pluto heard you, he thought you were one of the town boys who like to fool with him. He climbed up out of that opening to scare the wits out of anyone out there, and he sure did."

"I see," Thomas said sheepishly. "But I still don't understand how that sound could've been in the trees and in the tunnel under the house too."

"That's not hard," said Mr. Small. "Air currents caused it. This whole place is criss-crossed with tunnels and caves. Sound might travel a long way on a current of air. Mr. Pluto's bellows is a huge thing that can produce a mighty draft of air and the sound to go with it."

"Just an old bellows," Thomas said glumly. They were hurrying back across the lawn toward the house. Mrs. Small was stand-ing in the doorway waving to them to come even faster.

"We're going to be late if we sit down to breakfast," Mr. Small said.

"But I saw hoecakes, Papa, a mess of them!"

"So did I, Thomas," said Mr. Small. "So did I!" He began to run. Thomas sprinted along with him, letting out a whoop loud enough to be heard for a month of Sundays.

chapter 10

"It's the same,"
Thomas said. "I knew it would be. I knew
it had to be the same." Standing in the vestibule, he felt so glad it hadn't changed.

He recalled a time not too long ago when
he and his father had spent a quiet, talking
week together, camping in the hills and pines
back home. He could remember details of
the nights and days of that week, how the
woods had seemed smoky and close because
there had been so little rain. When they
were not hunting for their food, he and his
father lay low under the pines, where the
air was almost pure. Close to the ground,
where the earth smelled so sweet, Thomas
never wanted to let go of the fallen pine
needles. His father had talked and talked.
Later, when Thomas tried to recall what his

father had said, he couldn't. But now it came to him in snatches.

". . . may I talk to you about it, son? Our African church? The Negro church! . . . I can yield to its separateness when I realize that without it segregated, there would be no story of the Underground Railroad. There could be no sure refuge for the exhausted, runaway slave."

"That's the past," Thomas had told him. "That's no reason for the way it is now."

". . . through part of history, behind time or ahead of its time, it always reveals men strong enough to lead us out of the trap of any time. 'Go Down, Moses' . . . the singing of that was once forbidden. Think of it! Then it was sung by a whole nation!"

"Who sings it today?" Thomas had said. "Nobody listens. Great-grandmother stopped going to church even before the last minister left us. It's all over, Papa."

"You can argue, Thomas, I don't blame you. You young get stifled by its lecture and runagate Jesus. I won't deny its narrowness . . . but do you remember the Sunday school?"

"I don't remember any of it."

"The boys and girls?"

"Oh, yes, I remember how we would laugh, how we would cut up when we got tired of the lecture. And, yes, I remember the ladies."

"Those ladies in white, who would always volunteer to teach you," his father had said. "They could talk so about Jesus, until he never *was* a man."

". . . and the moonlight picnics. I remember them, Papa. And the hayrides. Why did they have to stop? Where did they go to?"

"Yes, you remember, Thomas. That's all I mean. The church is our treasure, son, our own true chance. And we are all the luck it has."

Maybe so, thought Thomas. The far-off voice faded out of his mind. Maybe not. He stood calmly, waiting to enter the small and stifling church. "It sure does feel good to be here though. It sure feels like home."

Mac Darrow was seated at the piano, playing quiet chords as the church members entered. Thomas wasn't surprised at all on seeing him there at the piano. Maybe it was true what his father had said about remembering the church, for slowly he recalled there had been a boy about the manner and size of Mac Darrow a long time ago.

He came when the last preacher came, Thomas thought. Yes, he was the preacher's own boy. He had a big, new piano and he didn't like us little kids touching it. But we would sneak into the church and touch it, we loved it so. I remember, I did that. He caught me and he told Papa and he never spoke to me after that.

Why is it bad boys bigger than me always play the piano so well, Thomas wondered. Why can't they sit back and be content with being bad? And big?

Like Thomas, Mac Darrow wore a dark suit. It wasn't a new suit, Thomas could tell, but it was a good suit and quite all right for Sunday.

Darrow wore a black tie. He had on black shoes that had a hard, high gloss.

He doesn't look like the same boy, Thomas thought. No, not at all like that boy hanging onto the black's tail.

As though sensing some stir in the congregation, Mac Darrow turned away from the piano toward the vestibule. He didn't look at Mr. and Mrs. Small nor at the twins. He looked at Thomas, and his hands never stopped moving over the piano keys. There was a playful flicker in his eyes as he recognized Thomas. Next he looked almost afraid of something, but then, that, too, was gone.

That's all right, Thomas thought.

He accepted the fact that there were certain things you didn't do in church. Even the most comic boy wouldn't laugh or make fun of it. Even the worst boy would not set flame to it, as some white boys had done at home, when the last preacher and his son began holding night meetings. To his mind, making fun and setting flame were degrees of the same evil.

Mac Darrow's hands were soft and sure over the keys. He looked at Thomas and through Thomas all at the same moment. He saw Thomas, but denied him.

I'm like that, thought Thomas. When I'm carving something from wood, I'm all by myself too. Mac Darrow could be my friend if he wanted to be, even if he is big.

The congregation had turned around to see. Thomas had known they would do that. The church was more than two-thirds full, and folks had turned around to look at Thomas and his family standing in the vestibule. Mr. Small searched out a pew empty enough to hold them all and far enough away from the pulpit so as not to take seats from the regular members.

Thomas waited to see if all those looks would be not unkind. He wanted to find out if the boys sitting like a rook of hawks close to the exit would lift their faces with some comment.

Their eyes flicked innocently over at Mac Darrow, but Darrow kept his mind on the hymns at his fingertips. He would not tell them how to behave, his bowed head seemed to say.

So they know about me, Thomas thought. They know about the house and that M. C. Darrow was fooling with me. But do they know we had a visitor last night?

The boys couldn't keep their curiosity hidden. They looked at Thomas with half-concealed excitement; Thomas was pleased by it. He tried standing straighter. He made himself look at them coolly, keeping his mind as empty of emotion as he could.

The women of the congregation—those ladies in white who would forever keep faith with picnics and Sunday schools—smiled fondly on the twins. Thomas had known they would. It wouldn't be anytime before they were asking to hold the boys or to sit with them on a Saturday. But it was those folks between age and youth that worried Thomas most.

They'll want to know what Papa has to offer them and what he intends to take away. They'll wonder what he's doing coming to their small church, because they won't know that the Black church, large or small, is all the same to him.

And they'll want to know if Mama is going to be just as regular as everyday or whether she will pretend she is too good for them. Mama is so pretty besides. She always will have the trouble.

The mothers and fathers of those boys sit-

ting hawk-eyed and shrewd in the far corner stared at Mr. and Mrs. Small. Mr. Small
nodded to them while going down the aisle.
He had spied seats about halfway to the pulpit, but at an angle from it, near one of the
squat, stained-glass windows. His nod was a
polite greeting and a gentle probe to see if
they would allow strangers among them.

Some folks nodded slightly. Others looked
long and hard. Thomas and his family passed
one pew where four big men were sitting.
Something about them made Thomas check
them in his mind. They looked alike, that
was it, and they did not wear suit jackets.
They were somewhat light of skin, with the
burnt look on their necks and cheekbones
that spoke of country and sun.

Farmers, Thomas thought. Maybe barn
builders. Why are they here today, without
their jackets?

They didn't look at Mr. and Mrs. Small nor
at Thomas or the twins. Their faces feigned
disinterest.

Thomas gave a silent whistle through his
teeth. By the time he sat down in the pew
Mr. Small had found for them, his hands
were sweating.

Thomas sat next to his papa. The twins
sat between Thomas and his mother. Save
for Mac Darrow playing the piano, there
had been almost a hush until Thomas and

his family sat down. Now people were again talking in the church; women were fanning themselves, for it was very warm. Thomas whispered nervously to his father.

"Did you see them, Papa? Did you see the four men?"

"Yes, I saw them," said Mr. Small. And understanding Thomas so well, he added, "Don't make too much of it. Don't let your imagination play with your sense."

"They wouldn't even look at us," said Thomas. "They were pretending we weren't even here!"

Mr. Small looked around. Folks were still staring at them while talking quietly. "That boy at the piano," Mr. Small said to Thomas, "he must be of the same family as the four men."

Thomas couldn't believe he had heard right.

"He's got the same head and the same build," continued Mr. Small. "Yes, they are of a family, five of them. One of the four is the father."

"But that's Mac Darrow at the piano," Thomas whispered. "That's the boy with Pesty and the horse yesterday!"

Mr. Small had been taking in and gauging the feelings of the people around him. He had expected people to be standoffish at first. You could assume that of country people in

the North, he told himself. He knew about
their clannish history, which gave little room
to strangers. But he hadn't expected folks
to be as cold as they appeared to be today
in church. When Thomas told him the boy
at the piano was Mac Darrow, he at once
sensed a hostility in the crowd. A moment
before, he had dismissed it as a product of his
own frayed nerves.

Now the minister entered and walked to
the pulpit. After him came the young people's choir, taking their position behind and
to his right.

He was a short man, the minister. He was
thin and not unpleasant-looking, Thomas
thought. The choir looked nice in blue robes.
They saw Thomas and his family right away
and they stared with simple curiosity.

The church grew still. There was the
sound of horses' hooves in the distance. A
lazy breeze filtered through the open window to the Smalls' pew. It hardly touched
Thomas before it died. The horses' hooves
were closer, pounding forward.

Something buzzed in Thomas' head; he
was watching the minister and the choir. The
minister seemed to be waiting. Looking
down at his Bible, he seemed to be listening.

The horses came to a halt at the side of
the church.

A horse? Thomas thought. Horses? Here?

Not more than half a minute passed, while all remained still in the church. The elderly women in the front row seemed to fan themselves harder. People looked down at their hands or their hymnals, but no one spoke.

What's he waiting for? Thomas wondered, staring at the minister. Why doesn't the choir begin?

There were noises in the vestibule. Thomas turned around, but no one else did, and he was embarrassed. The twins smiled up at him. They were settled and happy to be where they were, between Thomas and Mrs. Small. They were lulled into a pleasant frame of mind by the heat and stillness of this new place.

Down the aisle, past the Smalls in their pew, came Pesty in her outrageous pink-and-white costume and Mr. Pluto in his black cape and high hat. They made their way to the very first pew. Even though Thomas had known they were coming, he couldn't believe he was really seeing them.

Pluto seemed tired. Pesty led him along; his hand rested heavily on her shoulder.

There was a murmur, which ran from the back of the church forward. Folks around the Smalls' pew grunted to themselves angrily. The minister looked hard at them, and they quieted. He followed the progress of Mr. Pluto easing himself slowly into that first

pew—the old ladies there had moved far over
to make room for him and to avoid him at
the same time.

They don't like him, but the minister says
it's all right, Thomas thought. The minister is
going to preach to the devil, and the folks
don't like it one bit!

Pesty did not sit down. She went around
the pulpit, all daintiness, gathered a robe
folded on a chair and slipped the robe on.
Then she took her place in the very front
of the choir in the middle.

Why do they let her be in the choir—she's
too small, Thomas thought.

"Two hundred eighty-five," the minister
said. His voice was a startling, deep bass.

People stood up with opened hymnals.
Thomas grabbed a hymnal from the basket
attached to the seat back in front of him. He
gave it to his father. Mrs. Small had taken
another one for herself. They stood. The
whole congregation was standing, except for
the twins and old Mr. Pluto. Pluto was bent
over in his seat. From the rear, he looked as
though he might be sleeping. He appeared
tired out, not at all the man of the night before or even this morning.

Mac Darrow played beautifully. Thomas
recognized the hymn at once and smiled. He
didn't have to look at the words. Neither did

Mr. Small. They closed the hymnal, and then they knew why Pesty was in the choir.

It seemed to Thomas that Pesty's voice slid down from the ceiling, down the hot walls and into Mac Darrow's hands. It seemed to him that Mac Darrow's hands were inside the sound of the choir, holding on to Pesty's voice and then letting go of it when it became too strong for them. Her voice was like no other Thomas could remember hearing. It was pure and strong, not like a child's, and it was sweet and good, like a girl's.

"Over my head, I hear music in the air
Up above my head, I see trouble in the
air."

The congregation joined Pesty and the choir in a surge of new strength:

"There must be a God somewhere!"

The hymn went on and on. The minister sang part of it alone, with the choir and congregation humming softly. It was enough to cause chills to run down Thomas' spine. The minister had a voice finer than Pesty's, better than any voice outside of the stage.

Mama is sure to come every Sunday, Thomas thought. She will say Preacher has a voice good enough to speak with the Lord.

Through it all, Mr. Pluto sat hunched over as though not listening. He didn't move the whole time.

Thomas only half realized when the song ended, there was so much to watch and remember. He found himself sitting down and shushing the twins. They wanted more music. He promised them if they'd be still, there might be more in a few minutes. The choir had sat down. Pesty looked like a big doll in her long robe. Her bonnet looked pretty and not out of place. She was serious and sweet, sitting there in the midst of the older boys and girls.

The minister spoke solemnly of a God somewhere. Thomas listened for awhile. He talked about the Christian need to search out an invisible God in all things.

"Go to the rock," the minister said. "Tell the sinner who hides his face on the rock that he need not. No, he need not! Tell him that he is God. Say to him that the rock is God. Tell him to love himself and the rock and you, for God is with you. I say, inside of you there is God. Inside all of us, in all things, you will find God."

Thomas stared at the still form of Mr. Pluto. Mr. Pluto's head nodded, and his high hat rolled from his lap into the aisle. The minister paused. A man got up and gingerly returned the hat to Pluto. He did not smile at the still form nor touch it. The still form did not react as if anything out of the ordinary had occurred.

Is he sleeping there? Thomas wondered. Does Preacher mean to find God in old Pluto?

The minister droned on. Thomas stopped listening. He glanced out of the window. He could hear children playing somewhere down the street. They would be noisy until the church service was over, at which time they'd go home for dinner and more play.

Is that all they know how to do?

Thomas felt a little tired. The excitement of the new church, the new minister, was wearing off. Somehow it was becoming confused with past Sundays in church. Irresistibly his eyes were starting to close.

"Four hundred seventy-one."

Thomas woke up with a start. He couldn't tell how much time had passed, but automatically he stood up.

Why is church always the same? Awhile ago, I was glad it was the same.

Sleepily he tried to appear interested.

But why must it be so slow and boring!

Preacher walk, Preacher talk
Preacher eat with a knife and a fork.

The rhyme came to Thomas out of some
mean memory of a long morning.

> *I got a ticket to raffle*
> *I got two tickets to sell*
> *I got three pastors a-waiting*
> *To preach down in hell.*

> *Let the devil get ready*
> *Tell the devil his fate*
> *I got three pastors a-coming*
> *To pass him the plate.*

Pesty's voice quivered high above the choir,

"King Jesus lit the candle by the water side
    So all the little children could be truly
        baptized..."

Mr. Pluto got on his knees in the aisle beside
his pew. Thomas nearly choked. One of the
ladies in the front row stared at Pluto with
sheer malice. Mr. Small watched him with
grave concern. There was an angry stirring
in the congregation.

"Honor, honor, unto the dying day..."

One of those big men who must have been a
brother to Mac Darrow came forward and

tried, without touching him, to get old Pluto to get up.

"Darrow, sit down!" the preacher commanded.

"This isn't no Baptist place! Carrying on in the aisle," Darrow said. "We're Methodist here!"

"I said sit down! Mr. Pluto wants to kneel, let him kneel!" the minister said.

"So come along children and be
    baptized,
All the little children will be truly
    baptized,
Honor, honor, unto the dying day!"

When the hymn ended, the choir filed out. Pesty came forward and helped Mr. Pluto back into his seat. She squeezed in beside him and then watched the minister.

The minister was clearly upset. Thomas hoped he would forget his lecture and maybe preach around what had just happened. He didn't much care for old Mr. Pluto, but he decided he liked that Darrow man even less. Somehow he wanted the preacher to put the Darrow man in his place.

Instead, the minister turned to his Bible again. He grew calm and he read for a long time, hardly noticing the people looking out the windows.

Thomas looked up at his father. Mr. Small's face was bemused. Becoming aware of Thomas staring, he gently patted Thomas' knee.

All at once, Thomas felt totally let down. Everything had come to a standstill for some reason, he felt. All the hope of a new place—a new beginning and a new happiness—went out of him.

Nobody will come home with us. No one will laugh and talk with Papa. I won't have anyone to show my carvings to.

The church service was coming to an end. The collection plate was being passed around. They all stood to say the words that meant a parting.

"May the Lord watch between me and thee
 While we are absent, one from another, Amen!"

Mac Darrow disappeared through a rear door, the way the choir had gone, before Thomas had a chance to catch his eye. All those boys in the corner milled around their parents before they all filed out.

Thomas held one of the twins, while Mrs. Small held the other. The minister had not even welcomed them from the pulpit. Perhaps he had forgotten, Thomas thought.

But the minister did come forward to shake hands with Mr. Small. He was Reverend Breckenridge he told them, and he was pleased to have them come.

"You are a historian, I hear," he said to Mr. Small.

"Yes, I'll be working here for a time," said Mr. Small.

Folks were coming over to say a few words to their minister. In doing so, they were introduced to Mr. and Mrs. Small and Thomas. There were Henrys and Davises; there were Harrises and Browns. But that was all. If any of them had the least curiosity about Mr. Small leasing the house of Dies Drear, he said nothing about it. The four big men, those Darrows, filed silently out without a word even to the minister.

"You have yourself a good slice of history in that big house," the minister was saying to Mr. Small. "I've always admired it. I don't have a family, however, and I can't say I would care to live in it alone." He smiled pleasantly.

A warning? Thomas wondered.

"We had a good turnout this Sunday," the minister went on. "I haven't seen some folks who were here today in quite awhile. Mr. Darrow and his sons I haven't seen in a few months, although the one son, McDonald, plays piano for me each Sunday. It always

surprises me how good weather will bring
folks out more than anything I have to say."
He laughed, amused at himself.

Mr. Small watched him closely. "I don't
believe I've met the Darrows you speak
of. . . ."

"Oh, you will meet them. You will get to
know everyone—we are a small community
here. Folks are a little shy at first, but they
are good-hearted people. Awfully glad to
have you among us."

"Thank you so much," said Mr. Small.

"Good luck to you all, and I do hope to
see you next Sunday," the minister said.

Mr. Small told him he would surely see
them.

Outside some of the congregation were
still gathered, talking with one another. As
the Smalls emerged from the church, folks
looked down at their feet or away to the
street, as people will do when they are shy
and cannot think of what to say. Mr. Pluto
was just climbing into his buggy. He favored his lame leg considerably and fell heavily into his seat. Beside him was Pesty, and
she smiled at Thomas. On seeing Mr. Small,
Pluto touched his fingers to his high hat. His
mind seemed to be on something other than
passing the time of day with strangers. He
went off the way he had come, with Pesty in
the crook of his arms.

I'll not wave to them, Thomas thought to himself. I'll not wave at the devil, nor the devil's disciple!

Folks moved away, got into cars and went home. Mr. and Mrs. Small and Thomas, carrying the twins, walked slowly to their own car.

No one to come home with us, not even Pesty! No one to listen to Papa and hear about all the lives of history. What kind of place is this North anyway? What kind of a no-account place!

chapter 11

MR. SMALL decided they would combine lunch with dinner in the college dining room.

"It will be a Sunday treat for everyone," he said cheerfully. "Afterward, we'll still have time to find a locksmith."

He looked anxiously at Thomas. The boy wanted to meet young people, and there seemed to be no easy way to go about it. Thomas would need time to become adjusted; he would have to take things easy until the town had got used to them.

Mr. Small said nothing to Mrs. Small or to Thomas about the aloofness of the church members. He occupied them with talk about the college. Thomas forgot for awhile the mystery of the new house.

Mrs. Small was interested first in walking

the college campus and hearing about its
century-old history. They made their way to
the campus, and Thomas enjoyed walking
under the great oak trees. The trees made
the grounds dark with shade. Mrs. Small
liked the stone benches placed over the whole
of the campus, for she could rest often and
allow the twins to play in the grass.

"That's the main building," said Mr.
Small, pointing out the twin towers of the
oldest college building. "All the business offices are there, and a few of the classrooms.
I have my office in the left tower—would you
care to see it? You'll have to walk up. There
are no elevators."

Mrs. Small declined to climb so many
stairs. But Thomas wanted to find out what
it was like to sit in a tower. He and Mr.
Small climbed up and up. Finally they entered a corridor where Mr. Small opened
one of the closed doors with a skeleton key.

"This will be a cool place in summer," he
said to Thomas. "Ivy covers the windows,
keeping moisture close. Not much sunlight
can penetrate. But come the winter, I'll
probably freeze here."

"Isn't there any heat?" Thomas asked. He
had not much heart for talk. The climb up
to the tower had tired him; he wanted no
more than to go home to rest in his room.

"No heat that I know of," Mr. Small said.

"I thought colleges were supposed to be modern," said Thomas. "I thought up North they'd at least be heated."

Mr. Small had to laugh. "Now don't blame the North for everything," he said. "This isn't your state university with new buildings, sleek offices and central heating. Why this is history, son. Many of the buildings are much the same as they were a century ago. And if you don't mind, I'll dispense with heat any day for some good atmosphere."

I wish history would just die, thought Thomas. Why must Papa have it clutter up everything?

Mr. Small's office was not like any office Thomas had seen. It was like a watchtower, with garret windows and a musty smell. There were books piled everywhere, and bookcases lined the curved walls. An ancient desk by one narrow window had a small table on wheels next to it. Resting on the table was a typewriter that looked like an antique. The room was chilly, with a faint scent of cigar smoke.

"Nothing much ever changes in places like these," said Mr. Small. "Here there will be time to think, and time even to be bored."

"Papa, how is it you always know where to go so you don't ever have to change?" Thomas said glumly. He went behind the desk to see out of the windows.

Uncomfortably Mr. Small watched him, for Thomas had spoken in anger.

"I've had to adjust myself, too, to these new surroundings," Mr. Small said. He came quietly to the window. "It's not always easy at my age to begin life all over again in a strange place."

"Then why do it?" whispered Thomas. "Why bother when it's all the same anyway?

Out of the window, Thomas could see clear to the other side of town. "There are farms way out there, Papa. Look at that big one over there. They are plowing, even on Sunday."

A haze hung over the town and farms. If he stared a long time, the town would get smaller and smaller and then would jump back again in focus. Thomas tried to make it stay in place, but it kept on moving farther away and then back again.

He rubbed his eyes. "It keeps jumping at me," he said. "The whole town just keeps jumping around!"

"That's because you don't have a point of view," Mr. Small said. "Pick out a landmark and it won't happen."

"No, it'll happen if I was to pick out a landmark. I don't want to . . . it just doesn't like me looking at it. It just doesn't want me!"

"Thomas, that's childish," Mr. Small said. "You're tired. Things have happened too fast. Just hold onto yourself. Give the town time."

"I don't care anything for it," Thomas said. "You can keep it!" He spoke bitterly, and Mr. Small saw that he was close to tears.

"What is it, Thomas? What have I done to make you so mad?"

"I'm tired of everything being always just the same," Thomas couldn't help saying. He felt a sudden relief, as though somewhere inside him he had let fly a rock. "Always colored churches! Always white churches somewhere hidden! Why is it folks never get together? We didn't have to leave home at all. We could've stayed with Great-grandmother and had the very same change. We wouldn't even have to go to church, because there isn't any church left to go to!"

"Oh, I see," said Mr. Small. He looked out over the town. "I do see. . . . But you can walk any part of that town down there and nobody will stop you. A few folks might look at you hard, but no one will be vicious with you. No one will call you names."

"How do you know?" asked Thomas. "As long as there are hidden churches, how can you be so sure?"

Mr. Small was silent. He knew this town.

He knew that Thomas, his whole family, was safe in it.

But for how long? he wondered. And what about all the other towns, everywhere?

"You will have to try it," said Mr. Small. He knew what he said was not good enough. "You will have to walk it and see what happens." Nothing he could say would ever be good enough.

"Thomas, I wanted to take you to that church this morning because I thought it would be familiar. I thought it would be a good place to start to meet people and to make friends. You will have to give it time."

"Let's go eat now," Thomas said. "I'm hungry, I don't want to do anything but eat." He could not look at his father.

Thomas had turned from the window away from his father, when he eyes fell on something below one bookcase, where there was wood paneling. The thing glinted, and Thomas thought it no more than a pinpoint reflection when it jumped at him the way the town had seemed to. He sucked in his breath and stared. A cold fright passed over him.

"Papa," he said softly, "Papa, look there . . ."

Mr. Small looked and saw. He reached around Thomas for the object stuck in the wood.

"They are bold, aren't they, coming here

like that through my locked door?" said Mr. Small.

"Another triangle!" Thomas said.

"And they knew we would come here," said Mr. Small. "They knew I would show you my office."

"They who, Papa?"

"Whoever knows what I'm going to do before I do it. Whoever it is that has figured out my moves as though we, all of us, were pieces in a game of chess!"

"They could've been watching us for a long time," Thomas said. "Anyone hanging around up here in these towers could see anybody coming or going almost forever. It wouldn't take an awful lot to jimmy that door."

"You're right, of course," said Mr. Small. "I let the atmosphere, this whole morning, carry me off a little. Probably they have watched us from the time we left church. They may be close by even now."

"I don't like them," Thomas said. "I don't like them at all!" But his spirits lifted. At least folks cared enough about them to try to warn them out of town.

"Let's look at the triangle," Mr. Small said. He held it in his left hand while taking from his pocket one of the three they had found in the house.

Moving the new triangle around, Mr. Small

fitted it above the triangle he had taken from his pocket. Then he took from his pocket the last two triangles and fitted them to the first two.

"Papa, now we have all of it," Thomas said. "We have all four triangles and it's a Greek cross! But what kind of warning . . . what kind?"

"What kind indeed," Mr. Small said. "A cross made from four interchangeable triangles."

"Do you think there is danger?" Thomas asked.

"I have no idea," said Mr. Small. "In any case, danger usually doesn't come in the light of day. We won't worry about danger until nightfall." His manner was confident, and this pleased Thomas.

Mr. Small spoke matter-of-factly to Thomas. "Let's eat now and then find a locksmith," he said. "I don't like leaving that house all by itself for too long."

They ate, speaking not of the triangles or of anything that had to do with crosses or church or the house of Dies Drear. They'd eaten in the large, college dining hall. The hall had screened-in porches at either end, and they sat at a big, round table on the porch. There had been a pitcher of ice water on every table; Thomas had poured water for them all, even the twins. The twins had high chairs to sit in. The waitress had brought the chairs. She even brought the twins wood dolls to play with, since the hall was crowded with Sunday diners, and there might be a long wait for food.

It was the first time Thomas had sat down in a private room such as this, where there were white families eating just like his family. No one seemed to pay much attention at all.

Thomas felt so good he couldn't speak. Mr. Small watched him anxiously, and Thomas grew shy. After awhile, he looked up at his father, giving him a big grin. Mr. Small cleared his throat, chuckled to himself and studied the menu.

But they never found a locksmith. After a fine Sunday dinner of turkey with good dressing and gravy—Thomas had topped it off with Boston cream pie—they'd got into their car to begin the search.

"We'll go into the main part of town first," said Mr. Small. "See if anything is open."

They turned onto an avenue lined with trees. Xenia Avenue it was called. It extended from the college all the way through town.

"There's a library," said Thomas as they drove. He cradled the twins, one in each arm. They were tired now, hungry for the warmth of their bottles and their cribs.

"There's a drugstore and, look, a big church," Thomas said.

"That's the white Presbyterian church," said Mr. Small. "I know the pastor. He teaches a seminar on religion at the college."

"Can I go to that church sometime, Papa?" asked Thomas.

"You can go anytime you want," Mr. Small said. "We'll all go."

"Are Presbyterians like Methodists?" asked Thomas eager to talk.

"They are okay," said Mrs. Small, "but they aren't quite as good as Methodists."

"Mama!" said Thomas.

Mr. Small laughed. "Your mother's a Methodist from way back, Thomas. You'll have to forgive it. She can't help it if she's prejudiced."

"I'm not prejudiced," said Mrs. Small. "I simply have good taste."

Mr. Small threw back his head and laughed.

"I just want to try it," said Thomas, looking at the enormous, granite church. "Just to see what it's like inside."

Mr. Small stopped at the drugstore to get a Sunday paper. He made Thomas stay in the car so the twins would not want to get out. Mrs. Small stayed in the car also. He came back with candy and news that there was no locksmith in the town. There *was* the hardware store, which sold locks, but it was closed on Sunday. You might try the filling station, the druggist had said. All the Carr boys, who owned it, were handy with all sorts of things.

"It's surely a small town," Mr. Small said. "I love the flat way folks say things—not unfriendly but just flat, like maybe they all walked in from northern Kentucky in one big bunch."

"Where is the filling station?" asked Thomas. "I don't see it."

"No, it's on Highway 68 near the high school the druggist told me," Mr. Small said. "We'll have to go out there and talk to the Carr boys, whoever they are. Thomas, you'll get to see the high school, if it's that close by."

School, Thomas thought. I forgot all about it.

"Do I have to go to school tomorrow, Papa? Can I wait a few days until we get more settled?"

"They are still having Easter vacation here," Mr. Small said. "You have a few more days."

They drove a short distance out of town, away from the college on Highway 68. They passed a police station. To Thomas, it looked like a cramped chicken coop. There was one light-blue patrol car parked in front of it, with one policeman, who leaned against the car and looked sleepily across the highway. He checked their license plate as they passed and stared after them down the highway.

They found the filling station easily enough, for it was a large, well-attended and modern place. Mr. Small eased the car up close to the office. He didn't have to get out, for a big man came forward to see what he wanted.

"Afternoon," said Mr. Small, "Walter Small's the name—we've just moved here, in the old Drear place outside town. I need some locks and someone to install them. Can you help me out? Druggist said you might."

"I'm Carr," the man said. "The oldest boy. I have a few locks I can give you at a good price. Can't put them in until Monday though. All the boys is home with their families. Will that do . . . Monday?"

"Monday will have to do then," said Mr. Small. "Monday early morning, if it's all the same to you."

"All the same by me," said the man. "You have some vandalism out there?" he wanted to know. He was curious about them. His broad, white face was serious and intent on them.

"No," said Mr. Small. "No, nothing like that. My son didn't realize the kitchen door was locked when he stormed through it. While I'm at it, I thought I might as well change a few other locks."

"You intend to stay awhile then?" the man said. "The place has been empty for such a long time . . . I mean except for the old one called Pluto."

Mr. Small was cautious. He didn't want to tell the man too much. News spread like wildfire in a town such as this one. At the same time, he didn't want to give the impression he was hiding anything.

When he did speak, his manner was casual. "I'll be teaching at the college," he said. "We wanted space for the children. I thought I might do some farming on the side."

The man seemed to become more friendly. "You picked yourself a good piece of land for farming," Carr said. "Along that stream, the soil is rich as can be. I know, because that same stream meanders onto my father's land. Do you know his farm?"

Mr. Small said he didn't.

Carr continued. "Well, you can recognize it by the catalpa trees. There's a whole woods of them. Lots of berry patches in between them. Kids like to pick the berries. Get a good price for them, too, these days." He smiled at Thomas. "I know, I picked the same bushes when I was a boy."

"That right?" said Mr. Small. He started

up the car, hoping to ease away without appearing impolite.

"Oh sure," said the man. "Kids love playing there in the trees. My father, he's old now, and he never did mind them, except for the Darrow boys."

Mr. Small switched off the ignition. Thomas leaned forward.

"Darrow, you say?" Mr. Small said. He tried to appear only slightly interested.

"Do you know them?" asked Carr. "They have the closest spread to my father's. They're all around you out there. Mean ones, sometimes. Use' to bother that other old man—Pluto he's called. That Pluto and my father were young about the same time. My father, he was born in a log cabin in this town. But Pluto, he come here as a boy from somewheres. Seems to me I heard something about there being bad blood between the old man Darrow, the grandfather, and Pluto when they was young." Carr looked pleasantly at Mr. Small, pleased to talk on this slow Sunday. What he had to say appeared innocent enough. Of course, you never could tell about strangers, Thomas thought.

"The grandfather still living?" asked Mr. Small. He took out his handkerchief and wiped perspiration from his neck, then folded it neatly and returned it to his breast pocket. The gesture was slow and easy, giving the impression that he was tired and willing to sit a moment to talk.

"Oh no, indeed," Carr said. "He's been gone now, oh, seven, eight, maybe ten years. But he was a mean one. I know, I use' to play with one of the older boys. Old Wilbur Darrow. Haven't seen him in a couple of months though. They can stay out on that farm of theirs for six months at a time without folks seeing them. Always digging up trees and putting them back. When the grandpaw was living—he was River Swift Darrow—they moved the whole house a few feet to one side, looked around under it for about a week and then moved it back again where it was in the first place." He chuckled to himself, looking off down the highway.

"Sure, me and Wilbur Darrow were all right. The father, he was River Lewis, didn't seem to mind me. But the old grandpaw didn't like it. No sir, he didn't like me hanging around one bit. He'd come tearing out of that house calling me all kinds of rednecks. Now you know that can't be right. My family, we was always the same with everybody. We played no favorites and saw no difference."

"That's the best way," said Mr. Small.

"That's the truth, as I see it," said Carr. "No, they don't like folks hanging around.

Real secret they are. Always have been. They have a boy about your son's age. He doesn't seem to be as tough and sour as the rest. Maybe they're changing." He chuckled again. "Better watch 'em though. They got something in for that Pluto." Carr's eyes flicked away from Mr. Small's. "They're close by you, and I give you honest warning."

"Thank you kindly," said Mr. Small. He started the car.

"Got plenty good tires here anytime you need them," Carr said. "Plenty of good gas."

"I'll be coming back soon," said Mr. Small. Without effort, he imitated the flat, hill speech of the man.

"My young brothers like as not can fix most any busted thing. You let me know. They paint houses real well, folks say. We got a few tractors for plowing. The price of a field ain't high either."

"I'll be calling again," said Mr. Small as he drove out of the filling station.

chapter 12

"WELL then," said Mr. Small, "we know a little more than we did an hour ago." He headed the car back toward town, the way they had come.

"Carr people, Darrow people," Mrs. Small said, "I wonder what Mr. Pluto's family name is."

"Skinner," said Mr. Small.

"Who? How do you know that?" asked Thomas.

"I found out from the foundation, the first trip I made here—didn't I tell you?" Mr. Small said. "They told me his name is Henry Skinner."

"But is he the only Skinner?" Mrs. Small wanted to know. "Does he have family here?"

"I never thought to ask," said Mr. Small.

"I suspect the Carr man would have said something if Pluto had family here."

"You could find out," Thomas said. "You could go to the county seat maybe. They keep records."

"I don't care to find out," Mr. Small said. "Besides, Carr said Pluto came from somewhere else as a boy."

"And that there was bad blood between the old grandfather Darrow and him. I wonder why?" Thomas said.

"Time may tell," Mr. Small said. "Let's take things easy and wait awhile."

"Look," said Mrs. Small. "Look there, isn't that a school?" There was a drive off Highway 68 leading into an expanse of land, on which sat a sprawling, ivy-covered school. Mr. Small drove down.

"Oh, that's a pretty school!" said Thomas. It was called Washington Junior High and High School. It had a smooth lawn and a large playing field. To the right of it was a wide stream called the Little Miami River.

"Miami!" Thomas said. "That's in Florida."

"This whole area, both the town and country, is known as the Miami Valley," Mr. Small told him. "Some comical folks like to call it the Sinus Valley because it has so much rain and snow."

"Boy, I bet there will be lots of sledding,"

said Thomas. "I'm going to get me a big sled and whomp down every hill."

Mr. Small turned the car around and went back to the highway.

"I want to see the rest of it," said Thomas. "Please, Papa, I want to see the whole town."

The twins were quiet, almost asleep. Mrs. Small said they could drive around for awhile.

Mr. Small chose a street at random. On one side of the street was a white house the size of a mansion, with black trim. There was a huge lawn full of trees; there were swings and slides on both sides of the house.

"That's the grade school," said Mr. Small.

"What a lovely place for children to play," said Mrs. Small.

Thomas could see paper cutouts of Easter rabbits in many of the school's windows. He felt happy. Everything seemed normal again. He didn't even feel very tired. He looked at all there was to see and kept on feeling so good, he thought he would bust.

It was a pretty town. People lived in nice houses, large and small. Some of the houses were quite old, but well taken care of. They passed through what looked like a new section of town. Outside playing were many children still dressed in their Sunday clothes. Some houses had swings and slides in their backyards. Thomas thought they must be kindergartens, but, no, Mr. Small said, they were homes. People could afford good playthings for their children, he said. People made good money.

Thomas saw homes side by side where white and colored children played on the lawns together. And he saw houses on streets where you couldn't tell what kind of people might live in them.

They turned onto a back road leading through farmland. They traveled the road for some time. There were many barns with cows. There were fenced-in areas with hogpens and hog houses. Fields were plowed. Large pools of water stood like silver ponds along fence lines. The sun made them sparkle. The gentle wind made shallow waves over their surfaces. The air was so pure, Thomas could have laughed out loud. He poked his head out of the window, letting his face brush the leaves of trees by the road.

You could live here forever, he thought. Forever and forever. You could get a bicycle and let all kinds of dogs chase after you down these roads.

Soon they found themselves on the divided highway that passed by the house of Dies Drear.

"Time to get home," said Mr. Small. He looked at his watch. "Why, it's almost five-thirty! We've been fooling around almost the whole afternoon."

"I want to get to my room," Thomas said. "I want to take off these shoes and unpack my school clothes. I've got to register for school next week, don't I, Papa? I've got to get me my school supplies."

"I'll need to buy curtain material," Mrs. Small said to no one in particular. "Goodness, I'll need a lot of it for all those high windows."

"Buy. Buy," said Mr. Small. "All you think about is buying. Wait until I see some salary before you two start to buy."

"You're always crying 'dollar poor'," said Mrs. Small to him. "I know how much is in the bank."

"But you don't know which bank," said Mr. Small smiling. "I bet you don't know that."

"I do," said Thomas. "I saw the bank book on your dresser. The Miami Savings and Loan Bank, that's the name!"

"You're supposed to be on my side," Mr. Small told him.

"I have to get my school supplies," Thomas said. "I've got to be on Mama's side!"

Mr. Small turned the car onto the road leading up to the house of Dies Drear. The road had dried somewhat from the sun; in

another day, it would be completely dried
out. The sun lay above the trees on top of the
hill behind the house. The sky was almost
clear blue, with only the slightest sign of
night in it.

They grew quiet in the car. The twins
were sleeping.

"Poor dears," Mrs. Small said. "They can't
imagine what's happening to them."

They crossed over the bridge. Almost at
once, Thomas felt their isolation from all
things ordinary. They were so cut off from
the highway, from the town, from all life
that was normal, they might as well have
been locked in a closet. The dark and silent
house looming over them had already
reached out for them and was pulling them
in.

Thomas could feel it turning him cold all
over.

You've got to fight back at it, he told himself. You've just got to keep being warm inside and not let it get through you.

Like intruders, they went silently into the
house. The house seemed to listen to their
uncertain tread. It seemed to watch them,
pressing close as if trying to overhear. But
they were silent. Thomas and Mrs. Small tiptoed upstairs with the twins. The night-light
still burned in their room.

"Just take off their coats," whispered Mrs. Small, "and their stockings and shoes."

"These are their Sunday clothes, Mama!" Thomas whispered back.

"Do as I say," said Mrs. Small. "I don't want to disturb them by taking clothes off and putting clothes on."

Thomas did as he was told, although he didn't like it one bit.

Babies shouldn't have to go to bed in their Sunday suits, he thought. It's like they're ready to run away in case something bad happens—like they didn't belong here. This old house thinks it's going to get them—it thinks it's got us all on the run. I'll be patrolling this hall tonight. No sir, this old house will be sorry if it tries to scare my babies!

One of the twins whimpered in his sleep and shivered as with a chill. Quickly Thomas leaned over him. He covered Buster, putting his arm around him. Thomas stayed close until the child breathed silently, until the bedding was warm. Then he and Mrs. Small left the room, tiptoeing down the hall and down the stairs. They had looked from one closed door to the other going down the hall. They were on their guard.

Mr. Small stood in the doorway of the kitchen. The way he stood, so still there, caused Thomas and Mrs. Small to come quickly. He let Thomas through, but tried to bar Mrs. Small's way.

"You let me through," she told him. "Let me by."

"Don't look," Mr. Small said. "Please, let Thomas and me . . ." But Mrs. Small pushed by him. What she saw caused her to cover her face with her hands. A choked cry came from deep inside her. But that was all. She stood there without saying a word, with her eyes tight closed and her hands covering them.

Nothing Thomas could imagine, not all the devilment of strangers, of bad boys older and more daring than himself, could have prepared him for the sight of the kitchen. Looking at it, he was overcome with dread and loneliness. He reached out for his mother and put his arm around her. Mrs. Small swayed and leaned against Thomas.

The large sack of flour Mr. Pluto had bought for them had been emptied over the entire kitchen floor. It had been spread evenly in a layer, and over the layer had been poured water and apple juice. The whole mess had been mixed into a sticky, brown paste, which was spread over the kitchen table, over the stove and sink counters, over all the chairs and over part of the walls. The door of the frigidaire hung open,

and all the food there had been removed.
Whatever could be squeezed had been
squeezed onto the floor. What could be
poured had been poured out in swirls on
the floor. What dishes had remained after
Thomas' fall of the night before were broken
in the sink with the same sticky paste covering
them. The whole room, the windows, everything, glistened with this unspeakable icing.
Over it all was a warm odor of rotting food.
The only canned goods that had not been
punctured and emptied into the sink were the
cans of evaporated milk used for the babies'
bottles.

Thomas let go of his mother and took a
step into the room.

"No," said Mr. Small, "leave it be." His
voice was low, with an edge to it rough as
jagged rock. Thomas didn't have to turn
around to know what his face looked like.

"They mean to make us run with this,"
Mr. Small said. "They thought to terrify you
so," he said to Mrs. Small, "that there would
be nothing for us to do but run!"

"Oh, Walter," Mrs. Small whispered, "we
could move into town. We would be safe. . . ."

"Is that all we're made of?" he said. "Are
we to let fools run us out of this historic
house, our home? We're better than that, oh
yes! Whoever thought to make us run doesn't
know what we are made of!"

"Thomas," he said, "you come with me. Martha, you go up with the twins. Make bottles for them. Turn on the light up there if you want. Lock yourself in with them, but stay there until we get back. I'm going to get to the bottom of this right now. And before this night is done, somebody, some fool, is going to catch it!"

Mr. Small and Thomas saw her to the room. They made her lock the door from the inside before they left her. They had given her a small table lamp, which would give her light to see the whole room without disturbing the twins.

"All right now?" Mr. Small called through the door.

"Yes," she said whispering. "Yes, you can go."

"We're going. Don't be afraid. I don't think they will come back."

"Oh, I'm sure of that," she whispered.

She heard them leave. She wasn't sure of anything. But she took a deep breath and smoothed her hair behind her ears.

"All right, ghosts," she whispered, "come right on in! If you can work over my kitchen, I can surely work over your head!" She sat down to wait, with Thomas' baseball bat resting delicately across her knees.

chapter 13

BEHIND the house, Mr. Small slipped through the trees on the hill, much the same way Thomas had the night before. Darkness had fallen; there was no moon, nor any starlight to speak of. Instead of going up and over the hill as Thomas would have, he went around it from left to right. He moved swiftly, making hardly a sound. Thomas followed him closely. He couldn't see his father, but he could sense his movement through the stillness; he could feel the boughs settle back after his father passed.

We are Tuscaroras. He is my chief and I am his brave son.

Thomas had these thoughts and at once felt foolish for having them. Here they were about to fight off whoever it was had come to destroy his Mama's kitchen, and all he could do was imagine he was an Indian brave.

"Thomas, are you with me?" Mr. Small called softly.

"I'm right behind," Thomas answered. "Keep going."

"Wait. Shhh!" Mr. Small had stopped. Thomas came up to him, not even panting, although it was tiring keeping up with his father and walking silently at the same time. But he stood still and straight; he was invisible there in the dark, as was his father. Relaxed in the manner of the sprinter, his muscles were attuned for action.

Thomas listened. Always he had found it strange that sound could become caught within the random growth of trees. He could hear a truck on the highway. If he were standing on the veranda of the house, he might not hear it. When the truck sound disappeared, he listened again. Trapped there in the trees was the sound of someone walking. It was a soft sound of feet going back and forth and around, back and forth and around.

Whoever it was walking was not in the trees with them. The bed of pine needles would have deadened the footsteps. The sound was ahead of them and not at all muffled.

Is there an opening in these trees? Thomas wondered. An open place where they can ambush us?

Mr. Small had started again.

Thomas knew where to follow. Moving blindly, he would suddenly have the sensation that his father had left behind part of his spirit like a handprint in the air. Thomas would stumble upon this unsettled space and would know his father had passed there.

He had no idea where they were headed; he'd never been around the hill the way they went. He assumed his father had some plan and he hadn't thought to question what it might be.

They went down into what must have been a dried-up gully and then back up the other side. They went over a hillock that had a barren outcropping like a bridge. Covered with wet moss and fern, it was quite slippery. Once Thomas fell. There in the dark, he had the feeling he might slide forever.

Will they ambush us here?

When he scrambled to his feet again, they were back on the hill, with trees all around. A pale-yellow glow outlined pine boughs and tree trunks. It was enough light for Thomas to see the shape of his father a few paces in front of him. Mr. Small stopped again. This time he raised his arm motioning Thomas to stand where he was.

Thomas' muscles jumped and jerked beneath his skin. He was wet with the slime of moss and with his own perspiration. It was almost impossible for him to stand still, so ready was he for whatever lay before them.

If they ambush us, I'll swing up into the trees and jump down on them. I can do that a couple of times before they realize there are only two of us.

Then Mr. Small and Thomas were moving. They had walked a short distance when, without warning, the pale glow grew bright. The dense covering of trees gave way suddenly. They were indeed in open space.

They found themselves at the edge of a natural clearing and blinded momentarily by bright light. There lay before them a bed of flat rock, rectangular in shape, at the end of which was a cave. The cave mouth had heavy, plank doors. On either side of them were sconces, which held burning torches. The torches flared violently, sending smoke and a yellow glow up into the surrounding trees.

In the midst of it all, pacing back and forth like a falcon tired of his perch, was Mr. Pluto. He seemed in thought, and wasn't aware of them watching. He rubbed the back of his neck with one hand; the other hand was hooked in his belt.

Thomas couldn't quite believe he was seeing Pluto, the cave and those eerie torches, he had so prepared himself for danger and ambush. And something else, Thomas thought. The whole scene was suited for another place and time. Mr. Pluto should have fitted right in, like a bearded pirate perhaps, left in the wilderness by his fellow scoundrels. He should have been a part of these surroundings, Thomas thought. Only he wasn't.

Thomas couldn't quite catch on to what was wrong, but there was something about Pluto that kept jarring Thomas' mind.

Mr. Small started around the clearing toward Pluto.

"Mr. Pluto?" he called. "Pluto? I want a word with you!"

Pluto swung around, taking in the whole of the clearing. He must have seen Thomas and Mr. Small coming at him. His own face was in shadow caused by the torches above his head. But the rest of him was clearly visible. He looked massive, powerful, in the yellow light. Every inch of him recoiled in surprise. Still recoiling, he shrank toward the cave.

"Wait!" said Mr. Small. "You wait!"

But Pluto was gone. It wasn't possible a man his age and size could move so quickly, and yet he had. Like fluid pouring itself away, he was gone, leaving only the gaping doorway.

Thomas remembered the night before, and the way Pluto had lifted him off the ground. Again he thought what he had thought then: No old man anywhere, lame or not, could catch him from behind, let alone swing him off the ground.

Then Thomas was on to something. He didn't know what, but he knew what had been wrong with Pluto's pacing back and forth a moment ago.

"Papa, he wasn't sick at all. He was strong, did you see it? Papa, he was smoking . . . he had a cigarette!"

"I saw," said Mr. Small. His voice had that hard edge, the way it had when he had seen the mess in the kitchen. "And he wore new hide gloves like the first time. You bet I saw!"

Mr. Small tore one of the torches from its sconce and thrust it in the opening to the cave. He went inside, and Thomas followed. They were in a tunnel similar to the one under the house of Dies Drear. It ended some thirty feet ahead, in what appeared to be a room. Mr. Small threw the torch out the door, since the room ahead of them was lit. They went cautiously forward. And once inside the room, they stood against the wall next to the tunnel, looking all around.

"This is where he lives," Mr. Small said. "I've never been inside it, but there's his forge. And over there must be where he sleeps. The other tunnel entrance to the right must lead to the place where he keeps his horses. I do remember, he mentioned to me that there was an inner tunnel leading from this main room."

The cave was perhaps twenty-five feet wide and thirty feet long. The ceiling of rough and jagged stone was fifteen feet high. Thomas hadn't ever seen anything like it. One portion of the room was carpeted, with a large, worn armchair and a table for eating. There were photographs on the wall nearest to the table, and many yellowed calendars. On the other side of the room was a simple, brass bed. There was a pair of slippers placed neatly beside the bed, and flung across it was a robe.

What light there was in the room came from Mr. Pluto's forge. There was a fire burning, and his bellows rested on a tree stump next to the forge.

This was the first bellows Thomas had seen. He stared at it for a long time. He had known it would be large, but he had no idea it was such an awesome, strange instrument. A mighty bellows it was, old as an old man and tough and weathered as old Pluto himself had to be.

"Where the devil is he?" Mr. Small said. "He didn't come out the way we came in . . . so that leaves just two ways he could have gone."

Mr. Small crossed the room. There against the far wall was a ladder. Above the ladder in the ceiling, Thomas noticed for the first time, were two wood doors.

"Papa! Look!" Thomas said.

"Yes, I know," said Mr. Small. "On the other side of those doors is the platform you stumbled upon last night. It's a trap, you see. He built that platform just so he would know when folks were approaching. You always run into it before you expect to, even when you know where it is. That's why I came around the hill, so as not to be found out before I was ready."

Mr. Small climbed part way up the ladder. The doors were locked from the inside. "He didn't leave from up here."

"How about the tunnel leading to the horses?" Thomas said.

"You stay here," said Mr. Small, coming down the ladder. "If I find him, I'll bring him back with me."

He left the main cave and was back again in a minute without Mr. Pluto. "Looks like he has vanished into thin air," he said. "Maybe he is the devil, like you thought."

Thomas' father stood by the forge, with

his hands deep in his pockets. Thomas knew
he hadn't been serious about old Pluto being
the devil. But where *was* Pluto? And what
did he mean by running away from them?

"So there's another way," Mr. Small said.
"There has to be another way out."

"A secret way?" Thomas wanted to know.

"At least one he never let on to me about,"
Mr. Small said.

Thomas walked around the room. In back
of the table in the corner was a woodburning
cooking stove. The stovepipe went through
a metal plate attached to the wall above the
stove. There was more than likely a natural
opening to the surface ground, Thomas decided, that would allow the smoke to escape.
He put his hand gingerly on one round, iron
cooking unit in the stove. It was cold. There
was no fire at all.

"We'll wait for him," Mr. Small said. "He
has to come back. This is his home."

Thomas walked around and around. He
let into his mind everything he saw in the
room. He didn't touch anything there, but
he saw all there was to see, and closing his
eyes, he remembered where most things
were placed. Then, he stood still in the
room.

That's not it, he thought. You can hide
something pretty well by putting an object
in front of it. You have to know what you're

doing though. Most of the time, you'll just attract attention. The best way is to leave it out in the open. Leave what?

He spun around the room, taking in the bare part of the floor, that space between the table and the bed. He scanned the walls where the calendars and photographs left off. On the wall opposite, there were many harnesses, many lengths of rope, and some chain. There were clothing hooks. And on the wall nearest to the entrance, there were cooking utensils by the stove; below that Thomas saw a pile of firewood.

On the far wall, above which were the trapdoors in the ceiling, there was nothing save that ladder. And one, single length of rope almost hidden by shadow in the corner.

"Papa . . ." Thomas started across the room.

Mr. Small had had no intention of waiting all night for Pluto. He remembered his wife alone, locked in the big house. His anger came back, flowing into him cool as night air. He'd been looking the room over all the time. He had come to focus on that blank wall, just as Thomas had.

They both started toward the rope at the same time. It hung from a hook of some kind. Indeed, it was looped somehow, loosely, around an old clothes hook. Mr. Small moved the ladder over to it and climbed up, so

that his eye was on a level with the hook.
Just above the hook was a smooth hole. Mr.
Small saw that the rope came out of the
hole. And looped around the hook, it hid
the hole entirely. You wouldn't see it unless
you had a chance to stand, as Mr. Small was
now, looking sideways at it.

"This is it, Thomas," Mr. Small said.
Carefully he climbed down the ladder and returned it to its position against the wall. He
then took hold of the rope. Slowly it pulled
down and down, like a bell rope. When he
let go of it, it returned to its former position.

Between the ladder and the rope, the wall
began to slide. Thomas heard a grating
sound. It wasn't loud, but it was unpleasant,
the way the sound of rock rubbing against
rock can be. When it stopped, after a moment, that wall had slid back completely.
And what now lay before them was far beyond dream, or even nightmare.

Mr. Small took hold of Thomas' arm. No
matter how hard Thomas tried to pull away,
his father held onto him and dragged him
down.

"Lord!" Mr. Small whispered. "My Lord
in heaven, look at that! Look at it! *Look
at it!*"

chapter 14

THEY had to walk down into it. Considering that they were underground to begin with, they had to walk down into it from an unbelievable height. They had to walk down a wet, slippery ramp of chalk-white limestone, with enormous stalactites hanging just above their heads.

Mr. Small had to drag his son along. Thomas gaped at the stalactites, fearful that one might fall on him. He was terrified of the stalagmites that they had to walk through. He kept jumping away from them as though they were creatures from another world.

"You've seen them before, Thomas," Mr. Small said. "Get hold of yourself!"

All Thomas could think about was a fragmentary bit of information from an earth-studies class, which he had somehow filed

away in his mind: *Stalagmite: a calcium car-*
bonate deposit shaped like an icicle and
formed by the dripping of percolating cal-
careous water . . . Stalagmite: dripping of
percolating calcareous . . .

But he could not connect the phrases
with the monstrous forms around him. They
stood like sentinels guarding what had to be
one of the most stupendous caverns anyone
had ever seen.

Only no one had ever seen it, thought Mr.
Small. No one besides himself and Thomas,
and Mr. Pluto and Pesty, who sat down there
watching them come, waiting for them to get
there and to get on with it.

They took their time, Thomas and Mr.
Small. The knowledge that all of it had remained down there for a century or more
was almost more than Mr. Small's mind
could take at one time. So it was that he lit-
erally carried Thomas forward while, at the
same time, trying to hold himself back.

Once they had cleared the stalactites and
stalagmites, Thomas and Mr. Small were well
into the cavern. But they still had to go down.
They had reached a place much like a ram-
part arch in a staircase. They could stand
almost level; the limestone beneath their
feet was completely dry. But they still had
more of the ramp to walk to reach where
Pluto sat, behind a massively constructed desk.

It's Renaissance, Mr. Small thought, staring at the desk. The desk was dark, and elaborately veneered with fine woods. And it was decorated with the usual metal ornamentation of the period, although this decoration was far superior to anything Mr. Small had ever seen in a museum.

It has to be French Renaissance. Where the devil did old man Drear get hold of such an incredible work?

Mr. Pluto sat behind the desk with his profile toward them. He had propped one elbow on the desk with the hand under his chin and the index finger extended to his cheek. A brown woolen throw covered his shoulders like a cloak of gloom. It wasn't so much that he watched Mr. Small and Thomas come slowly forward, it was more that he listened and dreaded for them to come.

There is no war, Thomas thought. Mr. Pluto is the king!

The Lord of the Underworld! thought Mr. Small. This is a dream I tell you. It has to be!

But it was no dream. Where the ramp became dry, the cavern grew warm. Mr. Small and Thomas felt it at once, and it was a dry heat.

A uniform temperature, thought Mr. Small. A heat coming from the depths of the earth. Just warm enough, dry enough for all

this . . . this . . . wealth to maintain itself.
It's unbelievable!

At the end of the ramp, Mr. Small and
Thomas were in the midst of the cavern.
Barrel-shaped, the cavern rolled up and up
over them into an immense, vaulted ceiling.
Hanging on all sides were tapestries and Per-
sian carpets reaching almost to the floor.
There were row upon row of them, with
colors that leaped and glowed in the light of
torches grouped in the center of the cavern.

Mr. Small recognized in the carpets a color
massing and texture, and particularly fine
dye tones that one could find only in mu-
seums. He could believe easily enough that
an eccentric man such as Dies Drear had to
have been would possess them. What was as-
tounding was that because of the constant
climate in the cavern they were close to their
original colors and textures.

But why did he have them here? wondered
Mr. Small fleetingly. A source of sure and
easy money?

Whatever the reason, Dies Drear had
amassed and saved what was perhaps as fine
and complete a collection of decorative art
to be seen anywhere.

And that wasn't all. Between the rows of
hanging carpets and tapestries were whole
canoes, a few as long as forty feet, and whole,
richly painted, beautifully crafted totem

poles. Interspersed among these were carved and painted wood chests. They were Indian also. They had to be, Mr. Small thought. And piled atop them were blankets with similar designs.

He wondered what Indian people had painstakingly crafted such work. He didn't recognize any of it, although its value was obvious.

There were barrels upon barrels of silks and embroidered materials, which burst from the barrels and spilled out onto the floor. Mr. Small noticed some jewelry, pairs of shoes, watches, and chains of gold.

And there was more. One section of one huge wall was covered with glassware. Thomas stared at it. It was like a prism, for the glass came in colors ranging from aqua to deep brown and nearly black.

Thomas stood there next to Mr. Small at the end of the ramp, trembling all over. From the time they passed through the stalagmites, he realized they had discovered a place of great importance. Like his father, he had guessed rightly that they had stumbled upon the treasure house of Dies Drear.

The carpeting and tapestries were finer than anything Thomas could have imagined. They were hung very high up from oak cylinders, which had been polished a smooth, pale white. The cylinders hung on chains, which were suspended from hooks sunk into the vaulted ceiling. The rugs and tapestries were of varying lengths and sizes, and they divided the cavern into corridors of rich hues. In one shadowy depth of the cavern, Thomas noticed for a moment an enormous chain with links the width of three fingers. Some of the chain was wound around a winch, which had a lever attached to it. The rest of the chain rose up between tapestries to disappear in the murky darkness. With so much else to take in all at once, Thomas forgot all about it.

It was the glass that he couldn't take his eyes off.

"There must be a million bottles," he whispered to his father. His voice made echoing sounds, like many praying voices in a cathedral. He had to knot his hands at his sides to keep his arms from jerking convulsively. "Look at all the dishes and bowls and things. Why aren't they dusty? Look how they glow!"

It was true, the glass shone and sparkled.

"Some of it is as old as time!" whispered Mr. Small. "See how misshapen some of it is. Probably the earliest hand-blown glass you'll see anywhere."

Pesty, who all this time had been sitting on the arm of Mr. Pluto's great, carved chair, now rose and walked toward the ledges of glass. Suddenly there were hundreds of Pestys reflected in the glass. The sight of Pesty so perfectly reflected in so many different colors and shapes made Thomas dizzy.

There was a sliding ladder. Pesty hooked it into a groove on the wall above the glass. By climbing the ladder and pushing herself against a ledge, she could maneuver anywhere she wanted along the rows of glass. She demonstrated this for them now. She had taken up a cloth, and, ever so carefully, began to polish one thin-necked bottle.

Be careful! thought Mr. Small. Break that and you have smashed hundreds of dollars, you have let a part of history die.

No need for Mr. Small to worry. No curator anywhere could have handled the old and valuable glass with such delicate care. She looked over her shoulder at Thomas and smiled proudly at him.

"Mr. Thomas," she said. "This is my job to do." Then she placed the bottle back and came down the ladder. She took her position beside Mr. Pluto again. He had turned around to the desk to face Thomas and Mr. Small.

For the first time, Mr. Small was aware of the books in great glass-doored cases to one side of the desk. Some, oblong and yellowed, lay on the desk. Old Pluto had folded his hands lightly on top of them. Mr. Small stared at them, his eyes feverish with wonder, for he understood what they were. He stared at Pluto and then again at the ledgers; and he thanked the Lord that this old man, like Dies Drear before him and like himself, too, was a keeper of history.

Gently Mr. Pluto drew one of the ledgers close to him.

"An accounting," he said softly, his voice no better than a cry. He looked worn out—too tired, Thomas thought, to have had strength enough to mess up his Mama's kitchen.

"The day by day barter of black people," said Pluto. Sadly he smiled. "They weren't Mr. Drear's accounts . . . don't know where he got them. But they tell a tale or two. They show how mean folks had to be to buy and sell our people."

He stared dumbly at Mr. Small for a moment. Then he said, "I'm awful sorry I didn't stop to speak with your wife at church this day. But I felt so low there for awhile. I felt just like I was going to lay myself down and not get up. I've been sick you see. Yes . . . yes."

Vaguely Pluto looked around him. His old mind seemed to shift to something else. "I see you've found us out. I knew, oh yes. I knew you would when first you come over to see that house. Knew I hadn't long . . . all these many years, no one. And then Pesty. Old Little Miss Bee!" He laughed and folded the child in his shawl.

"Ain't it funny though, of all people, you can trust with a child? Never knew I could until one day she followed me in here. I didn't know she had until I saw her perched upon that ladder. I was so sure she would then tell Mr. River Lewis Darrow. I was sure of it, and that him and his boys would clear me out and clean this hall out. But no. I guess it is her plaything. I never know why she won't tell. But she likes to come here and I let her keep the glass. It is written down in the books that Mr. Drear was most fond of his glassware. Oh, Little Miss Bee and I can spend hours not even talking. Sometimes, I tell her stories about long ago, and she will fall asleep right in my arms."

Again Pluto's mind shifted. His eyes became frightened. He clutched at the ledgers on the desk. Pesty rubbed her head against his shoulder and put her hands upon his hands until he had calmed.

"They think because you're old, they can walk in and take over," Pluto said. "Isn't that right? They come around a-howlin' and pretending they're the ghosts. But they don't know, do you see? Little Miss Bee knows, don't you, my babe?" The child nodded. "Yes!" said Pluto. "Some nights them Darrows forgets about me, but there will still be signs of the old man and the slaves. I've seen him! I've seen them! Then my black horse, he will run with the wind, those spirits bother him so. I reckon they want to ride him, but he won't have nothing to do with 'em."

"Mr. Pluto," Mr. Small said softly. "Mr. Skinner. It will be all right."

Thomas felt awful inside. Looking at Pluto so old, so afraid, he thought suddenly of Great-grandmother Jeffers.

Why do they have to grow sick and weak? Why must it end like that for them?

He was filled with sadness. It was evil of him to have thought such a tired old man could be the devil. He could no longer see Pluto as king. And there *was* a war, but it was Pluto's with himself.

"We are sorry," said Pluto. "I mean I . . . we . . . hadn't ought to have fooled with you like that. Carrying on. Tricking you with stage magic . . ."

"Mr. Skinner, I wish you'd try very hard to make yourself clear," said Mr. Small. "Tricked us? You couldn't have had anything to do with what was done to the kitchen."

"No," Pesty said. "He means the other. He means about . . ."

But Pluto stopped her. "It was that I was

afraid, that's why we tricked you, don't you see?" he said.

"I thought sure them Darrows would just walk in and clean this place out if they knew how sick I was. They would find that sliding wall the way I found it, oh, years, years ago . . . What would it mean to them that slaves walked here, lived here peaceful, content no one was sure to find them? Here they were taught, the slaves were . . . yes, taught all the tricks and ruses old Mr. Drear could think up for them. And the good Jesus in heaven, he sure could think them up . . . the books tell it all! And they were taught the cross reading. They were taught . . ." he gazed around the cavern, "what wonder there is when men are free to see.

"It was all right when I was strong," Pluto went on. "They were always halfways scared of me. Their grandaddy, he was a boy with me. He was River Swift Darrow. He always said *his* grandaddy was a Mohegan by the name of River Thames. River Thames was supposed to have come down with Dies Drear from up East. And River Swift always said whatever was hidden when we hunted that house was his by legacy. I never said nothing when he said that, because I knew whatever it was was mine. I *knew* it. How did I know?"

Mr. Pluto laughed silently.

"Because what I hunted I couldn't put a name to. I couldn't have told you what it was I hunted, except it was inside of me. And I knew that house would bring it out of me and show it to me.

"River Swift, he hunted treasure. Sure that's all he knew to be legacy. But he was afraid of it, of that house," said Pluto. "So was his son and his son's son. He was scared to death, because the spirits knew he was evil and knew his sons was evil. But I wasn't afraid.

"No, not I," Pluto continued. "I grew to love that house. I got so I could walk it blind. All the tunnels. All the caves. But they was afraid, those Darrows. So the years passed, and they were afraid of me.

"I meant not to trick you, sir," Pluto said. His voice rasped, making a dried-up sound all about the room.

"It was just that if they were to ever know I be sick, they'd walk in out of the open. They wouldn't be halfways afraid of me being the devil at night.

"I see you are a historical man, an educated man," Pluto went on. He looked around him as though it was difficult for him to remember where he was. "I had no chance for education, but I do know hard thought in another. I am so sorry we had to fool you."

Mr. Small heaved a deep sigh. He could

make little sense out of what Pluto was talking about. He had so many questions, there was so much he needed to know. Gently he started to probe.

"Mr. Skinner, sir," he said. "I know you're tired, but just a little longer. Try to think about what I'm going to say. Can you tell me . . . is this the last unknown cavern? Is this the last uncharted hiding place?"

For a moment Pluto stared at Mr. Small and, then, looked beyond him. He bowed his head on his arms on the table. "We shouldn't have fooled you like that," he whispered. "It wasn't a proper thing to do. No. No. We had no right. No business!"

Pesty stood up straight, alert, also looking beyond Mr. Small and Thomas.

"Then again, as a historical man, perhaps you are not so all-fired proper," said a fierce, withering voice.

Mr. Small stood stock-still. Thomas couldn't have moved if he'd tried. It was River Lewis Darrow, it had to be. He must have followed them, waiting all this time.

Ambush, Thomas thought. How many sons with him? How many to handle at the same time?

"You just might be another branch of that Mohegan bunch, come here to steal from the storehouse and drive an old man half out of his mind!"

Mr. Small spun around. Thomas turned around ever so slowly. But what he saw was too much for him. The strength seemed to drain from his arms. No longer could his legs hold his weight. Not uttering a sound, he fell to his knees, unable to comprehend the phantasm before them.

For it was Pluto standing there. It was Pluto, who still sat slumped at his desk mumbling sorrowfully to the air, who, at the same time, stood in front of Mr. Small and Thomas.

"You!" hissed Mr. Small. "I knew there had to be another one of you!"

The Pluto who stood, nodded in recognition to Mr. Small. His beard and wild hair were golden in the torchlight. His eyes were wet and emerald green, flecked with gold sparks. He threw back his head and laughed and laughed.

No, thought Thomas. It wasn't fair to be a devil, to be able to divide one's self and have power over human beings. Now he understood everything. Pluto had spun all the tapestries, those carpets, himself. Pluto had blown all the hundreds of bottles, just by multiplying himself until he had enough Plutos to do the job. No wonder he was so worn out.

"No!" screamed Thomas. So terrified was

he that in another minute there might be a thousand Plutos, he began to sob.

"You devil! You hairy, green-eyed devil!"

He leaped on this second Pluto. He leaped high, before his father could stop him, catching the man about the neck. He wrapped his legs around the man's body and twined his fingers in that long, white beard. But Pluto was strong. He shook Thomas off like a lion shaking off ticks.

Suddenly Thomas flew through the air and hit the floor. By the time he pulled himself up to a sitting position, he was staring at his hands. His hands were gold and orange. His hands were covered with hunks of Pluto's beard.

"Get away!" he yelled. "Papa, it's stuck, it won't get away . . . Papa!"

Mr. Small tried to get hold of Thomas. "Son! Son!" he kept repeating. But Thomas was scooting all over the floor, trying to get away from his hands covered with the white beard. Some of it now seemed to be sprouting on his arms.

"He's turning me into a devil. Oh, Papa!" cried Thomas.

"Thomas Small!" The voice of the second Pluto boomed through the cavern like a hundred rushing voices.

Abruptly Thomas sat still. He looked up

at the strong, powerful Pluto towering above
him.

Ever so slowly, the Pluto raised his hands
to his face. He wore the now familiar hide
gloves, though only Mr. Small noticed them.
The Pluto began to speak, his hands still
poised there, near his cheekbones.

> "We wear the mask that grins and lies,
> It hides our cheeks and shades
>   our eyes . . .
> With torn and bleeding hearts we
>   smile . . .
> We wear the mask!"

With the most delicate motion, he peeled
away the corners of his face just below the
ear and let it hang in shreds around his
mouth.

chapter 15

"THOMAS, don't be afraid," said Mr. Small. "It's only a false face. Look. Look at it."

"It's stage makeup. You see, Thomas?" said the man. "There's a half-mask with the beard attached, which fits around my ears. There's the white wig and a dyed plastic substance that looks like skin. I had to add more beard with paste to make the mask fuller. That's why it came off in your hand."

"You could have got away with just the beard and the hair, you look so much like Pluto anyway," said Mr. Small. "Why did you bother with such difficult makeup? With the same green eyes, anyone would have been fooled."

"Yes, lucky for me my eyes are the same color as his," the man said. "I really didn't think you would be easy to convince. If I had to face you in the daytime, I wanted to resemble him as closely as possible. But you were on to me from the first, weren't you?"

"You said a few things out of place," Mr. Small said modestly. "Something about India in a way I'm certain Mr. Pluto wouldn't have said. And you wore those new, expensive gloves—they were a mistake, you see."

The man had to smile. "Yes, the gloves were wrong," he said. "I know that now. And when I saw you all there in the kitchen that night for the first time, I couldn't resist a bit of overacting. You were all so stunned, you see. But it was never my plan to terrify your son, then or now. Thomas, are you all right?"

Thomas had sat unbelieving through the conversation between his father and the man. Slowly he came to his senses. Not looking at the man, he rubbed the wetness of tears from his face.

"I knew no man as old as Mr. Pluto could catch me from behind."

"As it was, I had a hard time catching you myself," said the man.

Thomas was pleased by this. "Who are you anyway?" he said.

"I'm Mayhew Skinner. I'm my father's only son."

Thomas slowly shook his head, forcing

himself to understand that old Pluto had a son who looked just like him. "But why . . . why did you have to pretend like that?" he asked.

Mayhew had been kneeling in front of Thomas. He got up and walked over to the desk where Mr. Pluto now sat holding on to the ledgers. When Mayhew put his strong hands on his father's shoulders, Pluto looked up at him with all the hope he had left in him in his eyes.

"How were we to know what type of strangers you folks would be?" asked Mayhew. "My father became quite ill in January. He's had this running battle with the Darrows for as long as I can remember. But he was always strong, he could take it. I do believe he enjoyed the fight with them, since he alone knew about this cavern. He was certain they would never set foot into his cave, where he lived, as long as he could frighten them by being devilish. And he was right, they never did dare come too close. But when he grew ill, that all changed. He was desperate with the fear they might see how weak and sick he was. And when the foundation told him you folks would be moving in, he was terrified of what the Darrows might do to you."

"Then it wasn't Mr. Pluto who considered we might be an enemy," said Mr. Small.

"It was I," Mayhew said. He smiled grimly to himself.

"Calling my father the devil," he said. "As if being lame was a crime. Folks around here have been cruel to him for years—not only the Darrows. At least River Lewis believed he had a reason for *his* crime. Full of greed, he thought my father stood in the way of his legacy, which he believed was a treasure in gold." He looked around at the cavern. "I guess it is treasure of a kind." Sadly he smiled. "But not to my father, not to Drear.

"But let's get back to the nice Sunday-moaning church folks who never once cared whether my father lived or died. No, you can have them. They're the reason I left town. Even when I was small, I always hated them for their stupid ways. I guess I hated you folks before I saw you because I figured you would be no better than the rest."

Mr. Small glanced at Thomas, who stared at Mayhew Skinner with something close to awe. Thomas had never heard anyone talk the way Mayhew talked, at least not in front of his father.

"You shouldn't hate," Mr. Small said. "It will destroy you."

"That's a well-meaning lie," said Mayhew. "Folks have hated other folks for centuries, and the same business is still with us."

"Son," said Mr. Pluto, "please to tell him how it had to be."

"Don't worry, Father, I'm telling him," said Mayhew.

"You see, it was Carr who contacted me when my father fell ill," Mayhew was saying. "I live away from here. I'm an actor. I've lived away and worked since a long time ago, when my mother and I left this town for good. We had lived on that Drear property until my mother could no longer stand seeing the house *or* the town folk who thought we were strange. She loved that cave we lived in though. Odd isn't it, Mr. Small, that a son and daughter of slaves would find peace in the very sort of cave running slaves hid in?"

Mayhew didn't wait for Mr. Small to answer; he went on, his eyes seeming to go back to that long-ago time.

"You see," Mayhew said, "we lived on this land not conscious of the reason for our peace with it. We lived with a legacy we weren't aware we had. And yet we had a nameless knowledge of it, as my father has tried to tell you.

"We left it finally," Mayhew said, "but my father wouldn't leave. I blame him for that. I still blame him for forcing us to leave. He had grown obsessed with the tunnels, with the haunting figure of Dies Drear. He became fanatical about protecting the house and its history, and even its legend. I would say he is like you, Mr. Small, in his taste for what he calls our heritage."

"Indeed," said Mr. Small softly. "We always tend to belittle that heritage in our zeal to be free."

"I'll take freedom any day over all the romantic nonsense about slavery," said Mayhew.

"I mean not to glorify it," said Mr. Small. "I simply want people to know about it. It's a part of our history, and yet no one tells the truth about it."

Uneasily Thomas watched his father and this strange Mayhew. He couldn't take his eyes off him.

Uncomfortably Mr. Small and Mayhew Skinner glanced at Thomas. For his sake, they would let their argument go, for another day perhaps. Pesty sat down next to Thomas, as though to say that whatever sides there might be, she would take the one closest to Thomas.

"But to get on," said Mayhew, "Carr, the father, called me on the telephone. He said I'd better get back here, that new folks were moving into the big house. He said it looked serious—that you had obtained a job at the college."

"Serious in what way?" asked Mr. Small. "He didn't know about the cavern."

"No, of course not," said Mayhew. "And yet, he knew something . . . how can I tell you! He knew and respected my father. He knew the Darrows were after something to steal and he knew my father was hiding something from them. When Father became ill, and you folks were to arrive, he was worried. He understood that if my father was keeping something from the Darrows, it had to stay kept from them and possibly you, too."

"I see," said Mr. Small. "So we were suspect even before we arrived."

"Carr was afraid Father would have worse trouble if you folks turned out to be like the Darrows. I arrived here about three weeks ago. Then your furniture arrived. Father had made up his mind to trust you folks and decided to unload the furniture and place it in the rooms. I tried to tell him it was none of his affair, that he wasn't strong enough for it. He wouldn't listen. He never does. So me and the Carr boys fixed things up a bit."

"So then," said Mr. Small.

"You have to understand," said Mayhew, "we had more than one consideration. There was the foundation to think about also. They knew people searched for treasure on this property, but they had no idea why, or that the searchers were all one family. They knew the legend, that the house was supposed to be haunted. But they are sane people. How could they possibly understand the meaning of the legend to my father? To him, Dies Drear *lives!*"

"Did you know about this cavern?" asked Mr. Small.

"No, never," said Mayhew. "Not until a week ago, when my father decided he was mortal, like all of us, and thought it was time to tell me."

"Do you blame me, son?" asked Pluto. Sadly he looked up at Mayhew and Mayhew turned away.

"All these years," Mayhew whispered, "all this time, when there was this wealth . . ."

"It wasn't mine to touch, it wasn't mine!" cried Pluto.

"You say it is our heritage!" Mayhew's voice burst around them. "When all these years you've struggled and I've struggled. Yes, I blame you!"

"It was ours to hold, to take care of just the way the old man had," said Pluto. "But not to plunder, no, not to touch!"

Mayhew laughed without smiling. "How foolish, that history could be more important than men! No, of course not to touch," he said. "Father, do you have any idea how close you and Drear have become? He collected all this perhaps as a whim and he put it here, again perhaps, to save for slaves a portion of life which had been denied them. And you, Father, still save it, for, like a slave, you are bound to it simply because a troublemaker called Dies Drear says you are!"

"The man was more than just a troublemaker," said Mr. Small.

"To you maybe," Mayhew said. "To me he was a troublemaker who thought himself a prophet."

Mr. Small started to say more, but then seemed to change his mind.

After a time Thomas spoke up. "What will you do now?" he asked of Mayhew. "Will you tell the foundation about the treasure? Will you let them take it?"

Mr. Small waited. Mayhew looked at him, his eyes as cold and clear as glass. Then he looked down at his father.

"We could talk about it," said Mr. Small quietly, "if you'll allow me to become involved in that decision."

Mayhew nodded. "It's late," he said. "I'd better get Pesty back to the house, or they just might send Macky out looking for her. Pesty, are you ready?"

"I'm ready," she said.

"Then say good night to Father," Mayhew said.

Pesty went to old Pluto and threw her arms around his neck.

"Child!" Pluto whispered happily. "You'll come tomorrow, and maybe I'll feel like riding in the buggy. You want to still ride with a poor old soul?"

"I do!" she said.

"And remember," Pluto said, "not a word!" He put his fingers to his lips.

"No, never a word," she said. Sleepily she turned to Mayhew and held out her tiny arms to him.

Mayhew swung her onto his shoulders. "I'll take you as far as the yard," he told her. "I don't dare come closer. If they spy me, they'll think I'm Father."

Mr. Small looked at his watch. "Lord, it's late," he said, "and my wife is there, locked in the twins' room! I forgot all about her! Oh, I hope she didn't turn brave and venture out to clean up that mess they made in the kitchen."

"Something happened?" Mayhew asked. "What brought you all here so unexpectedly in the first place?"

"We came here, I guess, to accuse your father of trying to run us out of the house," Mr. Small said. "I was so mad, I didn't think much about it. I just got over here as fast as I could." Then he explained what had been done to the kitchen.

"What a bad thing, a sinful thing!" said Pluto. "They'll stop at nothing. Nothing!"

Trembling he tried to stand and nearly fell. Mr. Small caught him in time and braced him in his arms.

"Father, you're ill," Mayhew said.

"Let's get him out of the heat of this place," Mr. Small said. He helped Pluto up the ramp and out of the cavern.

In the cave, Mr. Pluto lay down heavily upon his bed.

"Ahh," he said, "I am tired tonight."

"You stay right here until I get back from taking Pesty home," Mayhew said to him. Pesty still rode on Mayhew's shoulders.

"Oh, son, I'll be all right," said Pluto. "I feel so much better just having Mr. Small know about the cavern. You see, he is a historical man, an educated man. He will know what to do with it all, Mayhew."

"Don't worry anymore about it," said Mr. Small. "Your son and I will take care of things."

Outside they slipped through the trees on the hill.

"It was them that did it to the kitchen," said Pesty to Mayhew.

"Which ones?" he asked her. "River Lewis, too?"

"No, not him," said Pesty. "After he seen Mr. Small at church, he told them to leave off. But they wouldn't listen. They was afraid that because he was a historical man, he would find the treasure before them. They think to scare Mrs. Small so she'd want to move into town. But not Macky."

"No? Macky wouldn't do it?" asked Mayhew.

"No," she said. "Macky, he told them he was tired and then he said to them that he was going to make a friend out of Mr. Thomas. He got slapped down for it, too."

Thomas was pleased to hear that Mac Darrow liked him. He was almost sorry the boy had got slapped for wanting to be friends.

But maybe it serves him right, Thomas thought. He did let me fall in the hole under the front steps.

He thought to himself that maybe Mac Darrow had a bicycle. If he did, they could ride around and have dogs bark at their wheels. He sure hoped Mac Darrow had a bicycle.

"So it was just the three of them," said Mayhew. "Wilbur and Russell and River Ross. They should be ashamed of themselves, acting like vandals on Halloween."

"You have any ideas on how to handle them?" asked Mr. Small.

"Call the police," said Thomas. "Just call the law and have them put away!"

Mayhew laughed to himself. "That would give me great pleasure," he said, "but taking care of them is easier than that. If their level is that of overgrown boys making mischief, then that is the way we'll have to treat them."

"How so?" asked Mr. Small.

"Let me get Pesty home," Mayhew said.

"I want to hear!" cried Pesty. "I want to know what's to happen!"

"You'll be in on it, good girl," Mayhew said. "Right now, it's time to run you home." He began to trot through the trees. Then he stopped and called back to Mr. Small, "You folks going to be up awhile?"

"I expect we'll clean up the kitchen," Mr. Small called back. "I'm much too wound up to sleep."

"Then I'll come by for awhile," Mayhew said. "I'll help you with the kitchen if you want."

"That's kind of you," said Mr. Small. "But hadn't you better get back to your father?"

"I won't stay long with you," said Mayhew. His voice was farther off. He was moving again. "I want to give you an idea of what I have in mind for the Darrow boys."

"Will you need our help?" called Thomas.

"Yes," Mayhew called back. "We're about to become a company of actors!"

chapter 16

"THOMAS, you and your mother are staring at me again," said Mayhew Skinner. He did not look up at them. "Mr. Small, why do you suppose they keep on staring at me?"

"They've never seen anyone like you," Mr. Small said. "Anyway, neither one of them ever looks twice at anything they don't like."

"Well, my goodness!" said Mayhew. "I wonder what kind of a 'thing' I am."

Mrs. Small had to smile. So did Thomas. They looked shyly at Mayhew. Here Mrs. Small had known him for only a couple of hours, and he seemed like a close friend.

Thomas couldn't keep his eyes off him. He wanted to know what kind of person became an actor. And how it was an actor used makeup and played different parts.

They were all in the kitchen, Mr. and
Mrs. Small, Thomas and Mayhew. It was
one-thirty in the morning, and none of them
felt actually tired. Mrs. Small and Thomas
sat at the kitchen table. Only Mr. Small
and Mayhew worked with the fury with
which they'd started. Thomas was scraping
the hardened paste off a chair, and Mrs.
Small was wringing a hot, wet dish towel
onto the tabletop.

Mayhew had organized them into two
teams. They were to use hot water to loosen
the caked flour and juice. Once it was loos-
ened, it wasn't difficult to scrape and wipe it
off the kitchen. Mayhew had the floor done
already. Mr. Small had cleaned the whole
sink, the refrigerator and the stove. Mrs.
Small and Thomas had done less because
they had to watch Mayhew and they had to
listen to what he was saying. He hadn't
stopped talking since he'd come back from
taking Pesty home. He still had a good part
of the false beard hanging from his face. He
had put the wig back on his head.

Looking at him covered with perspiration
and dirt from all the mess, Mrs. Small
couldn't help feeling sorry for him.

"Mayhew, why won't you take off your
jacket—it'll be filthy! That wig must be ter-
ribly hot. Take a break, both of you, before
you get sick."

"Listen to Mother," said Mayhew to Mr. Small. "There she goes, trying to change me already. Why do they always try to change us?"

"Because we're so perfect, naturally," said Mr. Small.

"That's right," said Mayhew. "No, they can't stand perfection, can they?"

"Both of you are just devilish," said Mrs. Small. Then she became serious suddenly. "Mayhew, how soon do you intend to leave here? Won't you stay awhile before going back to the city?"

Mayhew looked at her fondly and then turned away from her before he began to joke with her again. "There she goes," he said, "If I stay here one day too long, she'll have me enrolled in that college before I know what hit me."

"No, I wouldn't," she said. "Have you ever been to college, Mayhew? You might like it. I hear they have a fine drama department at the college."

Mr. Small laughed. "I suspect college drama would be like child's play to Mayhew," he said. "The only training he needs is good steady work."

"You're right about that," said Mayhew. "I'm up for a good part in a road company in another month."

"Then you'll stay here at least that long?"

Thomas wanted to know. "You'll stay here for a month more?"

Mayhew smiled. "I'll have to stay for awhile," he said. "We've got to get things straightened out here." He turned to Mr. Small. "I'll have to see what's to be done with my father."

Mr. Small stopped his work and sat down at the table on the chair Thomas had just finished cleaning. "Mayhew, take a break," he said. "Thomas, get him a chair from the parlor."

When Thomas came back with the chair, Mayhew sat down. Mrs. Small remembered she had half a jar of instant coffee packed somewhere in a carton. After a short search she found it. Quickly she made the coffee and they all drank it from paper cups, all that was left to drink from in the house.

They sipped the coffee, and Mayhew started talking again. "We have to decide a number of things," he said to Mr. Small. Mr. Small nodded. "But first we have to find out just how sick my father is," Mayhew said.

"He's an old man now," said Mrs. Small.

"Yes, but if he can get well," Mayhew said, "I mean, if there's nothing more wrong with him than fatigue and mental anguish—Lord, that's enough for an old man, surely! I have to get him to a doctor. Better yet, to a hospital and let them give him the once-over."

"Will he *go* to a hospital?" asked Mr. Small.

Mayhew was silent for a moment. "He's like all old people around here," he said. "Take them to a hospital, even mention that they have to go, and they're ready to lie down and die."

"Why is that?" asked Thomas. "Why would they be afraid of a place that can help them?"

"Understand," said Mayhew, "my father comes out of a time when people didn't have doctors. When there were no hospitals even halfway close-by. There weren't clinics. The only medicine people had they made themselves from alcohol and tree bark, roots and herb plants. And it was good enough. I don't remember him ever being sick, or my mother either. This is the first time in his life he can't take care of himself. It's killing him, knowing he has to depend on someone else."

Like Great-grandmother Jeffers, Thomas thought. She couldn't bear the sight of the traveling nurse who once tried to give her a hypodermic of penicillin. Great-grandmother had chased the woman out of the house, Thomas recalled, and had warned her not to come back soon.

How long has it been since we've been gone from there—two days? Just two days we've been here? It seems like a year.

"But you will have to get him to go," Mrs. Small was saying, speaking of Mr. Pluto. "If only to get him away from here so he can rest."

"Well, I have a plan," said Mayhew. "I'm chock full of plans." He laughed. "I'm going to tell him we've got to make the Darrow boys think he's so sick, he has to go into the hospital. Then they will make their move to find the treasure. It's not really a lie. Once they see him leave, they'll be over here under cover of darkness before you have time to blink.

"I'm going to call Carr as soon as it's morning," Mayhew said. "He'll have to make arrangements to put Father in the hospital." He glanced around at them sitting there. "You folks are going to have to do for Father, because no one can know that I'm here."

"What do you want us to do?" asked Thomas.

"Everything," said Mayhew. "I'm going to hole up in that treasure house of old Mr. Drear's until it's time to come out. First off, we will make a show of getting Father to a hospital. We could take him by car, but I think we'll call an ambulance. Then, Thomas, you and Pesty will let it be known he is in the hospital for a week or so . . . or at least until tomorrow, depending on what's wrong with him."

"I get it!" said Thomas. "You want them
to think they've got to move tonight, I mean
the night that's coming, because they can't
be sure Mr. Pluto will be in the hospital
more than twenty-four hours."

"Right," said Mayhew. "I want to get the
Darrows over here fast, before they have
time to think too much about it. And I'm
going to have Pesty let them know Father
became very excited, making himself sick
over something Mr. Small found belonging
to old Dies Drear."

"Oh, I don't know," Mrs. Small said pen-
sively. "Are you sure we're doing the right
thing? Shouldn't we just call the police on
them, have the law reprimand them good,
and leave it at that?"

Mayhew glanced at Mr. Small, and Mr.
Small nodded ever so slightly. "Martha,
there's more to it," Mr. Small said. "There
are things you don't know about . . . let Mayhew do it his way."

Thomas was about to ask what it was they
didn't know about. So was Mrs. Small. But
Mayhew turned away from them in that sad,
alone way he had. In the last couple of hours,
Mrs. Small had seen him do this many times,
as though there was something weighing
heavily upon him. Whatever it was, she knew
it was not her business to speak of it.

Thomas understood this too. There was

some secret, he imagined, that involved Mr. Pluto, Mayhew and the Darrows. His father knew about it.

How was it his father always knew more than everybody else, he wondered. Mayhew couldn't have told him anything more than what he had told all of them, because they'd been together, all of them, from the time Mayhew returned from taking Pesty home.

So then, Thomas thought, it's something Papa has figured out from what has already happened. I'll have to wait to find out, if I'm ever to find out.

"It won't be easy getting Father to go to the hospital," said Mayhew, "but I think Mr. Small and I can convince him. We'll make excitement out of it. We'll tell him we can't work the stage magic on the Darrows until he is gone."

"Whatever you plan on doing," Mr. Small said, "please don't use this house to do it in. I don't want the Darrows here or near my little boys."

"No, of course not," said Mayhew. "You needn't worry about them getting in here anymore. There's only one way they could have got in to do their work on this kitchen. Why is it Father never told you about that hall mirror?"

"What?" said Mr. Small.

"You mean the mirror right out there beside the parlor door?" said Thomas.

"There's a tunnel behind it," Mayhew said.

"How is that possible?" asked Mr. Small. "The mirror hangs between the parlor door and the front door."

Mayhew explained that the parlor wall was a false wall, about a foot and a half short of the outer wall of the house.

"The corridor between the false wall and the outer wall leads down to the tunnel," Mayhew explained. "That tunnel is parallel to, and to the right of, the tunnel under the front steps."

"Are the two tunnels connected?" Thomas wanted to know.

"I believe they are," Mayhew said. "At least they used to be. The tunnel behind the mirror has several branches, while the one beneath the steps connects only with the kitchen, for the purpose of hasty concealment. The mirror tunnel goes under the stream at the foot of this property, onto the Darrow property and the Carr property. I would guess a long time ago, nature started the tunnel. But then men, probably slaves helping Dies Drear, expanded it to the two properties, where there were farmers friendly to runaway slaves."

Thomas shivered. To think he had slept

in that parlor because he thought it would be safer than his room upstairs! He could have been carried off by them and hidden in the tunnel!

"My goodness!" said Mrs. Small. "That handsome mirror . . . and all the time . . ." she couldn't finish the thought. She, too, shivered as with a chill.

"Yes, and you'd better remove the mechanism," said Mayhew. "It's at the base of the mirror—here I'll show you, Mr. Small, because if your twin boys like to crawl around, they might find it and easily get into the tunnel."

They all went with Mayhew to the hall. There he kneeled down and felt around the bottom frame of the mirror. "Here it is," he said. Mr. Small bent down to get a close look. Then Mayhew released a lever, and the mirror swung gently out.

In front of them was a dark, narrow corridor, which slanted steeply down below the foundation of the house. Thomas could clearly hear running water.

"Whoever came here last night most surely removed his shoes," said Mr. Small. Squeezing himself sideways, he made his way down the corridor and peered into the tunnel.

"He had to," said Mayhew, "else your carpet would have been soaking wet.

"This tunnel is never dry," he said.

"There have been several cave-ins below the stream, and I would suggest you not allow Thomas ever to walk around in here."

He closed the mirror, and he and Mr. Small worked on the mechanism until they had removed it.

"That's a relief," said Mrs. Small. "Goodness knows, I don't think I'll ever be able to look into that mirror without feeling a bit strange."

They returned to the kitchen but Mayhew declined to sit down. "I'd best be going now," he said. "You folks ought to get to bed, get as much sleep as you can."

"Yes," said Mr. Small.

"I'll come back here early," Mayhew said, "dressed like my father, in case anyone is watching. I'll do business with Carr from here and then I'm going into hiding."

"But what is it we are going to do with the Darrows?" Thomas asked. "When will we begin our show?"

"Once we get Father in the hospital, we'll have the whole day to get ready for them. You're going to do some shopping for me, Thomas. Mr. Small, you might have to take him to Columbus. It's the only city close-by that I know has a theater supplies store large enough to have what we are going to need."

"I'll be glad to," said Mr. Small.

"Do I get to wear a costume?" Thomas wanted to know.

"I'm afraid you'll be wearing mostly rags and chains, Thomas," said Mayhew. "I'm sorry to say slaves were never very keen dressers." He grinned.

Thomas was awfully disappointed. "Not even a false face?" he asked Mayhew.

"Oh sure, you can have a false face and a false head of hair, if you like," Mayhew said.

Thomas felt better and he smiled.

"What do I get to wear?" asked Mr. Small.

"You're going to look swell," laughed Mayhew. "I've got you all set for a black fire-and-brimstone suit and shoulder-length, gray-blond hair."

"I can hardly wait," said Mr. Small smiling.

Mrs. Small looked a bit peeved, but she didn't say anything. Mayhew, noticing her expression, winked at Mr. Small.

"Now what is it, Mother? Are you feeling left out?"

Mrs. Small wouldn't say anything.

"You want to be an actor, too?" Mayhew said.

Mrs. Small's face lit up. They all burst out laughing.

"I'll have to get one of the Carr girls to look after your little boys," Mayhew told her. "Will that be all right?"

"Oh, that will be fine!" said Mrs. Small breathlessly. "What . . . I mean . . . who do I play?"

"Well, there's nothing that says one of those slave ghosts couldn't have been a woman!"

"Oh no, really!" said Mr. Small.

Mrs. Small covered her face and giggled into her hands.

"You can't do that," Thomas said. "Old Dies Drear wouldn't have sent a woman back into slavery."

"Sure he would have," said Mayhew.

"And he probably did, too," said Mr. Small. "Many times women slaves could pretend they were house servants out on an errand, when actually they were running away."

"But the Darrows would never believe it," said Thomas. "I mean, I bet they think of ghosts like I do—that they are men."

"Maybe you're right about that," said Mayhew. "We could shave her head perhaps."

Mrs. Small gasped. Mayhew and Thomas laughed uproariously. "No," said Mayhew, "we can do better than that. We'll make you a man, like Thomas. We'll have to build you both up with muscles. Tell me, Mrs. Small, do you think you could manage a pair of men's shoes with wood blocks attached to them?"

"Do I have to?" she asked.

"If you want to be a ghost, you'll have to do what Mayhew says," said Mr. Small.

She thought a moment. She, like Thomas, had an urge to act. "I rather fancy myself more of the lace and satin ghost-type," she said. "However, I will wear men's shoes and muscles if you all promise never to tell anyone!"

"We *don't* promise!" they all said in unison.

And then Mayhew Skinner took his leave of them. Mr. Small let him out the kitchen door. Mayhew paused there a moment before leaving. That look of sadness, of loneliness, they'd all seen before passed over him. He looked at each of them in turn, his fierce, green eyes turning suddenly soft.

"I adopt you as my family of rascals," he told them. "I adopt you, each and every one." And with a flourish of his arm, he disappeared into the night. Without a sound, he went and was a part of it.

Now how do you suppose he does that? thought Thomas. I wonder if before he goes away, I could get him to maybe teach me how to melt away like that!

chapter 17

"I HAVE lived these caves for fifty years. I have lived them when no one cared but the damp and dark. And now you come here telling me how to be and how to die. No, I'll not let them steal. I'll not leave. I'll not go to any hospital!"

So old Pluto spoke. They all stood around his elaborate desk, Mr. Small, Thomas and Mayhew, watching him clutch at his ledgers. It was splendid night in the cavern of Dies Drear, although it was nearly midday outside. The burning sconces, grouped like a fiery bouquet in the center of the cavern, flared high. The rugs and tapestries leaped and glowed in a fury of color. Mr. Pluto's green eyes were alive and dreadful, with pinpoints of light. His great black cloak fell around him like a shroud. No one of them dared come too near him, for, at the moment, he was almost mad with fear.

"Father," said Mayhew softly, "Father, listen, I have been trying all morning to tell you."

"You be still!" screamed Pluto. "You just keep yourself still! I allow you to come here —you think on that! I allow you here, all of you. This is *my* house to hold and to keep as long as I live. And no tribe of thieves, whether they be educated or fools, is going to steal it!"

"No. No, this time you are wrong." Mr. Small spoke evenly, hardly letting his voice rise above a whisper.

"You!" hissed Pluto. "You are a thief after all. You thought to fool me to get at this storehouse, but you'll not do it. No, it's mine to hold and to keep!"

"No, not yours," said Mr. Small. "If any one of us were to tell, the foundation could come claim it at any time. They own all this land and these caves, too. It's not yours, it's no man's."

Mr. Pluto seemed to sink down into his shroud. He was still, breathing heavily. Mr. Small thought to walk near, to see if he were all right. He hoped the old man was all right; he gambled on the strength and will of decades to come hold the old man up now. He had no intention of destroying Pluto. He had meant only to somehow bring an end to his utter fear and dread. It was cruel, what he had said, for the cavern of Dies Drear should have belonged to Pluto, since Pluto alone had cherished it for so long.

"We mean not to steal one thing in this cavern," said Mr. Small. "I mean that we want nothing here for ourselves. All we want to be sure of is that the Darrows or anyone else should never waste it. What would become of the fine tapestries, the great goblets and bottles, if one day some men bought this property and decided to dig deep for wells or what have you? Anything at all could cause all of this to be destroyed. Do you understand what I'm saying? At any moment, at any time, all of this could be buried forever!"

Slowly Pluto raised his head. "Buried?" he whispered. "Sell this . . . my land?"

"Not your land," Mr. Small said. He held himself tight inside. He made his heart cold so he might speak what he felt he had to. "You are a squatter here, old man. You have been paid to be a grounds-keeper, and that is all you are here. You have no rights whatsoever."

"No, not true," said Mayhew. He came around Mr. Small and walked behind the desk where Pluto sat. He went to one of the cases that held the ledgers and old, rare books. Carefully he pulled down one large book, in which there was much handwriting on paper that was thick and deep brown.

"Here we have the last will and testament of Dies Drear," he said. "Care to look at it, Mr. Small? Well, no need for you to. The man had some kind of premonition—like a prophet, he knew his time was near. And he willed this cavern and whatever was found in it to the first son of slaves that was able to find it. He knew no bounty hunters, nor any other white men, would ever find this cavern. For the one who found it would have to have been cut off from his past, his history, as were the slaves. He would have to find that past in order to find himself. It took my father some thirty years, but he found it."

There was silence in which Mayhew handed the book to his father. Ever so carefully, old Pluto laid it atop the pile of ledgers on his desk.

"I wasn't looking for this place, nor no treasure," Pluto began. "You see, Mr. Drear built another wall in my cave where I live. Not the wall you see now, with the ladder and the rope hanging down. No, not *that* easy to find this. But he built a wall to look like any cave wall, with a bit of dye like a covering of seeping dirt, or maybe just a little grayness for to make it seem ordinary. How many years I stared at it because I had nothing else to look at! It was my picture screen, on which I placed my dream of finding something . . . I didn't know what. Then I began to dream of finding something belonging to those who were sold and those who were brave and sold all the same."

"Because your ancestor was one of the two slaves who died the week Dies Drear was killed—is that it?" asked Thomas.

"No," said Mayhew.

"No, not the two slaves that was hunted and killed just the same as the old man," said Pluto.

"But the one mentioned just once in all the history and the legend told of the house," Mr. Small said. "There were *three* slaves caught the night two of them were killed."

"The third slave!" said Thomas. "He got clean away!"

"He got away," said Mayhew, "and he went far north, reaching Canada, where he lived and prospered until he died."

"And his great-great-grandson came one day to claim all this," Mr. Small said quietly. "Maybe he had heard some ancient tale about something hidden in this house. A tale that had been passed on from generation to generation, each time becoming less clear and more mysterious."

"Yes," Mayhew said, "but the slave who ran free wasn't the only slave who ran free the time the house of Drear fell silent as a tomb. This cavern had at least one slave still resting within it. He could have been Mohegan, as the Darrows say. The bounty hunters who caught and killed two of the three running slaves and killed old Drear never had an inkling of this cavern. They never even found that first cave. But at least one slave had to be in here. When he, too, ran free, he told a tale of hidden wealth, which, as you say, Mr. Small, became distorted through generations of telling. By the time River Swift hunted the house of Dies Drear, what he looked for was hardly more than a wish."

"You've got to try to understand," said Pluto. "River Swift, he wasn't so awful bad. He was my companion when we were young. We shared the dark and dank of the tunnels—our footsteps together made hardly a sound on those ghostly paths. I suppose in the beginning he hunted for himself, the same as I did. But always he was a greedy boy, greedy to have and greedy to take. I reckon he got to thinking hard about old Mr. Drear dying wealthy as a king. So over the years, what he hunted got changed into a stake of glitter all for himself. By the time his manhood came, he knew there was a treasure of gold some place. He would have laid out his footsteps on my back to get to it, too. But you shouldn't blame him to his soul. We both lost, he and I. We both did lose . . ."

"So then," said Mr. Small, "we have all of it now."

"But listen," Mayhew said softly, "let him tell it—it has been so long that he couldn't tell it."

And Pluto told them, his voice going back to that hopeless time.

"After the boy and his mother had picked up and gone," Pluto said, "I had nothing to look at but that wall, night after night and year after year. Until one time, I got so I couldn't stand to look at it. So I got me some paint and I was going to paint the whole cave white. I started with that wall. I painted the whole wall that night and then I went to sleep, glad I had done something to take my mind off the tunnels. I had walked them so often, finding things—clues, bits and pieces of the cross. . . ."

"Like this cross?" said Mr. Small. He produced the four triangles he and Thomas had fitted into a Greek cross. Very carefully, he put the cross in Pluto's palm.

Pluto stared at it. "It's just a one they will make to pretend with," he said. "Them fool Darrows. The cross was handed down to them just like the tale of the Mohegan was. But they don't know how to read it . . . they don't know what's it's for. Just mindless, they will make the cross and stick around the triangles."

"How do you read it?" asked Mr. Small. "How can you read from four triangles that are exactly alike, that can be moved to fit any angle of the cross?"

There was a pause in which Mr. Pluto's fingers moved over the cross. He looked up after a moment and smiled at Mr. Small. "Old Mr. Drear surely did fool you with this one!" he said. He chuckled. "First, before I read it, you must tell me how you found it, Mr. Small."

Mr. Small explained how he had found three triangles stuck in the doorframes inside the house and the last one in his office in the college tower.

"Thomas and I found that by moving them around, we could make a Greek cross out of them."

"Surely you did," said Pluto, "and that was your first mistake. Now wouldn't you know Mr. Drear would figure out that folks, not knowing what they saw, would move a triangle when they came upon one? Wouldn't you know he knew folks well enough to figure they would have to touch it, turn it over, hold it up to the light and turn it around? Yes! And he counted on them doing that.

"You can't move a triangle from where you find it! You can't move it if you want to *read* it!"

"So, not moving it, how do you read it?" asked Mr. Small.

"This was a cross reading for fleeing slaves," Pluto said. "It was Mr. Drear's own creation. It's all written down and diagrammed in one of his books. He gave the crosses to the people who helped slaves from one hiding place to another. They were called the Conductors, I believe, and it was rare that a slave ever saw them. But a slave would find their crosses. And what he found weren't fancy crosses like this one and others Darrows will make. Those a slave found might be made from twigs tied together and nailed up. Or even dead animals fixed on a tree trunk.

"The first thing a slave was taught about the cross reading was that he would never find a triangle laid flat—not on the ground or anywhere else flat. It wouldn't read, because you could move around it, and if you could move around it, you couldn't get the sense of it.

"The second thing a slave knew was that a triangle could be found on any object perpendicular to the ground—a cliff wall, a riverbank, a tunnel wall, a tree. Anything at all, as long as it was upright and stayed put.

Then, when he found a triangle, he had to stand directly in front of it.

"The third thing a slave learned was never to touch a triangle he found. He was to stand directly in front of it, but never to touch it. If he touched it, he might change its position in some way and upset the reading.

"Next, he would imagine he could make two lines leading from the two legs where they made a right angle. And with his finger he would lengthen these lines until he had himself a cross. The place where the triangle he found fit on this cross would tell him where to go next."

Mr. Small pulled out the paper on which he had drawn his first diagram of a triangle. With dotted lines, he extended the two legs of the angle until he had made a perfect cross.

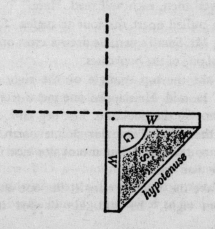

"That's it," said Pluto. "That is how it was done."

After a moment he continued. "The last thing a slave was taught was never ever tell the cross reading. Not to another slave, not to a freeman, not even to his kin. That's why so few people ever heard about it. Slaves took the reading to their graves. That's why, whenever I chance to pass a graveyard and see all them crosses, I can't help but pause awhile, just looking."

After a time Mr. Small spoke. "Please read for me now, Mr. Skinner, the metal and wood cross the Darrows made."

Pluto held out the cross in his palm. "This way, with the four triangles in place," he said, "the cross reads nothing. But pull the cross apart and look at one triangle at a time . . . well then, each will read. Here."

He pulled apart the four triangles. Then, using Mr. Small's pen, he drew a cross on the side of one of the bookcases.

"Take the top triangle on the right side first," he said. He slapped one metal triangle in place on the bookcase. The peg sank deep into the wood. "One leg points north, the other to the east. That means flee east from where you found it.

"Take the second triangle, the one on the bottom right," he said. He slapped it in place. "One leg points south, the other to the east. Flight is south."

He placed the top left angle on the outline of the cross. "It points north and to the west. You must flee north.

"And the bottom left angle will point south and to the west." He placed it, completing the cross. "The flight is west."

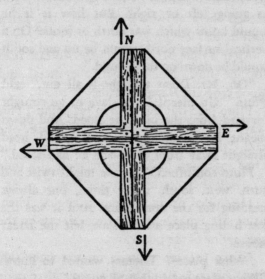

Thomas and Mr. Small stared at the finished cross with eyes that could see it as running slaves must have seen it.

"What a wondrous thing," Mr. Small said, "to read freedom from so simple an object as a cross."

"Yes. Yes," said Pluto. "And a slave might find ten different triangles made from sticks, animals, even bits of rags, in one single night of running through woods, along streams, tunnels. Each time he came upon one, he would stand before it, make the outline of a cross and continue on."

"I can see how he would know east or west," said Thomas, "because that's the same as going left or right. But how is it he would know which was north or south? On a vertical surface north would be up and south would be down on the ground."

"Oh, Mr. Drear thought it all out," said Pluto. "Up meant for a slave to go straight forward from the place he stood. And down meant he should turn around and head straight away from the place he had stood."

Pluto continued. "A slave might twist and turn, west, south, many times, but always heading for the same place. And it was the last hiding place after a slave left the Drear house."

"What place?" Thomas wanted to know. "What place would they all go to?"

Mr. Pluto stared at him. So did Mayhew.

"Why, the Negro church, son," said Mr. Small. "The freeman's church. A slave might hide among its congregation, and no hunter could find him. Wherever the church was, the pieces of the cross would lead him to it."

"Father, it's getting late . . ." said Mayhew.

"You trying to hurry me?" Pluto said. He looked hard at Mayhew. The talk of the cross, and the fact that he could read its meaning when not even Mr. Small could, had seemed to strengthen Pluto.

"What was I speaking about?" he asked them. "Where was I?"

"You were talking about painting that cave wall," said Thomas, "and then I think you said you lay down."

"That's right," Pluto said. "I did lay down and I did sleep. I don't think I dreamed about a thing that whole night. You don't know what rest that was for me—I was plagued by nightmares. Old Drear, he used to visit me there in my sleep. Sometimes, oh, in the dead of winter, sometimes he would come and even wake me up with his noise. Scare me so. But not lately. No, it's like he knows I am old and tired."

"Father . . ."

Pluto waved his hand impatiently at Mayhew. "So then I slept good that night and woke up the next morning ready to work with whatever came to my mind to do. Sometimes I had to make my own work. But the first thing I saw was that wall. It was like I never even painted it. The color, that grayness of dye the shade of shale or seeping limestone, it just bled right through my

white paint. And then I knew. I touched the
wall, and it came off gray, dirt colored, onto
my hand.

"But there was no way to move that wall,"
Pluto said. "There was no trick to it. No. I
had to build me a hammer made of iron and
I had to pound that wall down. I pounded it
down and carried its chunks and bits away by
the bushel basket. And I buried that wall so
no one would know. It took me a long time.
I used to work at it only at night, only
when I was sure I was safe. When it was done,
I found that other wall where there was still
a few strands of rope hanging in the corner.
I fitted another rope in, oh, ever so carefully,
and when that was done, I pulled down on it
and I found all this."

"All this," Mayhew said quietly to Mr.
Small. "And it *is* his. It is."

The splendor of the cavern made them re-
mote and separate within it. Mr. Small gazed
around, taking it all in as though he would
breathe it into his lungs.

"You understand that you can never claim
it," he said to Pluto and Mayhew. "You do
know, don't you, that no court of law I know
of would ever honor the last will and testament of a dead abolitionist to the great-
great-grandson of an unnamed slave."

Mayhew smiled. There was that look of
sadness, of loneliness absolute in his eyes.

"We would fare worse than any Indian tribe trying to make honest claim to a legitimate treaty," he said.

"Oh yes, we know," said Pluto. "We know. We know."

Thomas couldn't translate all he felt now into any kind of thought. Standing there in the quiet, splendid beauty of the cavern, he was speechless. He was awe-struck by this old Pluto, who was king after all, who lived only to keep a treasure he couldn't bear to part with, which would never belong to him.

Mr. Small sighed. I'm afraid I don't have much heart for scaring Darrows," he said. "It all seems so foolish now."

"Foolish?" said Mayhew. "No, not foolish. You feel that way because you have stood in this unreal place—this unnatural house which doesn't exist—listening to a story that shouldn't have happened, told by a man whose steadfastness is not believable."

"But we are here," said Mr. Small. "The story is true, and the man is true."

"It's all a dream," Mayhew said. There was that mocking look in his eyes, the look of stage magic. "The Darrows are the point, and fooling them is the game. Don't forget our actual world out there of silly deeds and simple wants."

"But does Mr. Pluto have to go to a hospital?" Thomas asked. "Can't he just stay right here where he is?"

"I'm not going to any hospital," Pluto said. "You can't make me go!"

"He could stay here," said Mr. Small, "right here. Sleep here until we are finished with the Darrows."

"Father, will you do it? Will you sleep here and not come out until we are finished with them?"

"Until you do the stage magic," said Mr. Pluto to his son. "Like you explained to me this morning."

"That's right," said Mayhew.

"Now why is it you think you can play me better than I can play myself?"

"Now, Father . . ."

"You answer me," Pluto said. "You just go ahead and tell me how it is. I been the devil Pluto for more years than I can remember, and you think you can do him better than me!"

"I don't want you to get sick," Mayhew said. "I know you can do it, but it will be dark—we might have to wait half the night."

"He's going to play me better than I can," mused Mr. Pluto. He turned his old, angry eyes on each one of them. "No, I won't do it. I'm going to sleep in my own bed tonight."

Mayhew heaved a deep sigh. Once he opened his mouth as though to argue further with his father. But then he shrugged and shook his head.

"You are stubborn, mean and the devil for sure," he said to Pluto. "All right. You play Pluto, but on one condition."

"What one?" asked Pluto.

"That you see a doctor as soon as this is over. This week for sure."

"I don't have to go to any hospital?"

"Not as long as you see a doctor, but you will do whatever the doctor says when you see him. Will you agree to that?"

"Oh, I don't suppose it will hurt," Pluto said. "There's nothing wrong with me that a little more rest won't cure. I've got some good medicine I fixed myself only last month. I'll go see some doctor, let me see, about Friday or maybe Saturday. Does that suit you, boy?"

"That will be fine," said Mayhew. "I'm going to tell Mrs. Small of your promise. She will see you get to the doctor on time."

"Now," said Mr. Small, "I would guess you will need to take my place in our play for the Darrows."

"I'd better," said Mayhew. "I'll have to be there to make sure Father doesn't terrify them too much. You can be a slave with Thomas, Mr. Small."

"What about my mother?" said Thomas. "She won't have a part."

"Maybe we can give her the job of getting us ready," said Mayhew. "Maybe that will satisfy her."

"It will have to," Mr. Small said. "I'm rather glad she's not going to be in it. If I know her, she'd give it all away."

"So then," said Mayhew, "we are ready to begin. It's almost afternoon. Father, we'll leave you for now. I have to get my stage magic together."

"What makes you so sure you can fool Darrow with it?" said Pluto. "You didn't much fool Mr. Small here."

"He fooled me for a longer time than we'll need to fool the Darrows," Mr. Small said.

"Anyway," added Thomas, "he didn't have me to help him, Mayhew didn't. With me to help him, we'll fool them good."

"Let's go to the cave," Mayhew told them. "I have some materials there. I'll tell you of my plan."

Thomas was so excited, he could hardly think. It was going to be scary, what they would do to the Darrows. He had no idea what the scaring of them would be like, what Mayhew had in mind.

But I'm going to be an actor, he thought. Maybe I'll be good at it, too!

chapter 18

IT SEEMED to Thomas
as though they had waited for hours. He
couldn't see a foot in front of him where he
lay in the trees surrounding the clearing.
He was not to talk, nor could he move very
much. This scaring of the Darrows wasn't at
all like he had imagined it earlier, when it
was still day. Now he was chilled through
to the bone, lying low on his stomach in the
pitch black night. He couldn't see his father
where he, too, lay in wait, a short distance
away. He couldn't see Mayhew or Mr. Pluto,
nor hear them either. All was so silent, so
mysterious, he had to clench his fists to keep
his teeth from chattering.

Why don't they come? he thought. What
are the Darrows waiting for?

Thomas could feel small insects crawling

over his ankles, where the chains were locked. He wanted to sit up and slap the bugs, but he dared not.

"Don't you think of moving," Mayhew had warned him. "They might wait in the trees for an hour or two just to make sure no one's around. If they spot us before they hit that clearing, the game will be over."

Thomas heard the slightest movement. He buried his head in the pine needles. He had phosphorous tape over his eyebrows and around his eyes. The same tape outlined his jaw and his cheekbones. He had to keep his head always down, so as not to glow there in the weeds and bushes.

He thought, I'm getting scared. I'm going to be just scared awful if one of them happens to step on me.

Think about something else, he told himself. Think about today.

Whatever sound Thomas had heard was no longer separate from the subtle sounds of night. Thomas let himself become full of the day and all the preparations they had made. They'd run into the Darrows once, Mr. Small and Thomas, and it had been a tense meeting. It had happened after Thomas and Mr. Small returned from Columbus, where they'd spent a lot of Mayhew's money in a theater supplies store.

Never had Thomas been in such a place. There were costumes and masks, some of which they bought. There were trunks full of drapery material, and shelves of cosmetic paints and dyes. There were whole stage sets, with fake platters of food and crystal glasses painted to look as though they were filled with red wine. Mayhew had asked them to find gossamer wings. And they had been lucky to find a huge, feather-light pair, which they purchased at a fair price.

Thomas was still talking about the store when Mr. Small stopped the car downtown to do more shopping. They bought groceries and dishes to replace temporarily those which had been broken. When later they were coming out of the hardware store, their arms full of paint-mixing pails and such, they saw three of the Darrows coming toward them.

Thomas stopped in his tracks.

"Keep yourself moving away from the car," Mr. Small had said out of the side of his mouth to Thomas. They had not bothered to cover up any of their purchases from the theater supplies store.

The Darrows appeared to be just as surprised to see Thomas and Mr. Small. One of them stopped in the street, looking around at the other two, but the two biggest ones came on ahead.

Mr. Small said good day to them in a matter-of-fact tone, since it was the custom always in a small town to speak to everyone. The Darrows looked hard at them, and then one said good day. He tried to smile and did manage a weak one.

"You be Mr. Small?" the one Darrow had said. Thomas remembered it all.

"That's right," said Mr. Small. "I don't believe I know your name."

But the Darrow man wouldn't say who he was. He went on talking, looking not at Thomas or at Mr. Small but at the store wrapping paper that partially covered the paint pails and mixing sticks.

"Getting ready to paint things," Thomas couldn't help saying with a broad grin. "Going to paint the whole inside of the house."

Mr. Small had given him a sharp glance, telling him not to say anything else.

"Hear you folks had some excitement over there in the big house," said another one of the Darrows to no one in particular.

The Darrow who had spoken first looked menacingly at his brother.

Mr. Small smiled at them. "Oh, you mean old Pluto," he had said. "Yes, he took real sick in the night. We had to bring him to Columbus, where there is a good doctor I know. We left him there with a colleague of mine, since he wouldn't go into the hospital. He has to have a thorough going over, but I suspect he will be coming back home tomorrow morning."

Then Mr. Small avoided looking at them, giving the impression he was hiding something.

Thomas began to hum significantly.

The Darrows fidgeted nervously. "That's all?" one of them couldn't help asking.

"Why, what more could there be?" said Mr. Small. "Everything has been so peaceful and quiet, even with Mr. Pluto becoming ill." And then he bid them good-by. He and Thomas left the Darrow men gawking there in the middle of the street.

Now Thomas grinned at the dark, his mouth pressed against pine needles. He opened and closed his hands resting at his sides, trying not to rattle the chains attached to his wrists. By now, he was cold and stiff in every muscle. He shivered from head to foot, for he wore only a flimsy tatter of a shirt and trousers that were mostly rags. The fronts of both had been brushed with phosphorous paint. He still lay in the position Mayhew had placed him a few hours before to hide the glow of his clothing.

I can't stand it much longer, he thought. I'm going to have to move in another five minutes, I can't help it. I just can't!

Mr. Small, close by Thomas, was having similar thoughts. They had waited three, maybe four hours. The time had to be well after midnight, and he wondered how Thomas was faring there, hidden in the weeds and bushes.

He won't be able to stay still much longer, Mr. Small thought. He must be cold with so little on. We'll all be at the doctor's before this is over.

Mr. Small was dressed much like Thomas, in tatters and rags, with chains about his wrists and ankles. The chains were real and quite heavy; Mr. Small hugged the ground in the way Thomas did. During the long period of time he lay there, he began to feel as though he *were* a slave hiding and running. Somewhere in the back of his mind was emptiness and fear; loneliness, the way a desperate slave would feel. At the same time, Mr. Small felt slightly ridiculous. The whole business of the night, having to lie so still, hardly breathing, was a bit mad. But Mayhew Skinner had a way of making the unreal and the unaccustomed seem normal.

He's a magician, pure and simple, thought Mr. Small. I wouldn't have believed a week ago that anyone could get me out here, catching pneumonia just to perform an elaborate practical joke. What have we come to, acting like fools!

But Mayhew had his mind on something entirely different. For one thing, he was burning hot. He could feel perspiration trickling down his neck onto his shoulders, then down his arms. He, too, lay on his stomach, hidden by trees and grass and bushes. He was dressed in a heavy, odd-fitting, old-fashioned suit. He wore a long, blondish wig streaked with white, which fell to his shoulders. The wig had been treated with a phosphorous spray paint, and the effect of it in the dark, when he removed his hat, was spectacular. His face and neck were covered by a cream-colored mask, fitting over his skull under the wig. Never had he imagined that one day he would play the part of a white abolitionist. He didn't find the prospect funny at all, however. He would play his role with all the grim skill he had. He fully intended to be the most superb apparition of all.

Slowly Mayhew lifted his head about an inch, just high enough for his eyes to scan the top of his father's cave across the clearing, directly above the wood doors in the cave mouth. Hidden there, among the trees, was Pesty.

Poor baby! he thought. Has she fallen asleep? I should have my head examined for letting her stay out here. They'll become suspicious.

He had tried to provide an alibi for Pesty

staying out late this night. In his best fem-
inine hand, he had written to Mr. Darrow,
and had allowed Pesty to deliver the note saying that the child wished to stay in the big
house until Mr. Pluto returned. The child
was unusually upset over Mr. Pluto's sudden
illness, the note had said, and the Smalls
would be pleased to have her stay the night,
if Mr. Darrow did not object. Darrow had
not replied, and Pesty had come anyway,
since she always went where she wished and
returned home when she felt like it.

If she falls asleep, we're sunk, thought
Mayhew.

Lying the way they were, facing the clearing and the cave, neither Mr. Small nor
Thomas, nor Mayhew either, had any way of
knowing if the Darrows were creeping about
among them. Pesty was to watch for them
and give the signal because, being the kind
of child she was, she knew enough about
night and Darrows to know when they were
moving.

Then Mayhew heard it. Just a soft sound
it was, like a bird giving its last weak chirp
before sleep overcame it. The sound came
from above the cave. It was Pesty's signal.

Mayhew grinned uncontrollably.

Come on, Darrow. Come on in.

Mr. Pluto was calm and comfortable. He

sat within the cave tunnel, just beyond the partly opened plank doors in the cave mouth. He rested in a cushioned chair Mayhew had provided for him. Wrapped snugly around his shoulders was his heavy brown throw. Upon his head was his black stovepipe hat. He played no man but himself and he was the same as always, except for Mayhew's warm, hide gloves on his hands and a wool blanket bunched around his legs.

Pluto could see the whole clearing and the trees surrounding it, without being seen himself. But he couldn't see Thomas or Mr. Small or Mayhew. He had stared at the clearing and trees for hours; he knew the three of them lay out there, but, after a time, he began to think maybe they'd gone and left him. Maybe they had tricked him, and an ambulance would burst suddenly into that clearing and take him away.

Halfway through the waiting, the staring, he had become afraid. The night settled around him; the minutes hung inside him in even lengths of cold. He felt his mind getting further away from him. He became frightened that he might see the real ghosts of old Mr. Drear and the two slaves, as he had seen them before when he was sick and tired with despair. There had been a time when what he saw was just the Darrows walk-

ing stealthily behind him, never too near
and never too far away. They had followed
him down the years, as had those ghosts, so
that, oftentimes, he couldn't tell which he
was seeing.

But now his mind settled back. He had
caught hold of one thought he had tried
earlier to fix in his mind. He could even doze
off now and again, sitting in the chair with
his chin resting in his beard. But always that
one idea stayed close to his ear; that much of
his mind was alert and ready.

He dozed.

If I do nothing more, the thought went,
I'm going to fix up those Darrows once and
for good!

He opened his eyes. He hadn't heard
Pesty's signal. At least, he didn't know if he
had. But darkness was moving ever so carefully back in the trees and from three directions. Darkness was making just the gentlest,
swishing noises in the pine boughs.

Without effort, Pluto stood up. Straight
and tall he was, easing the chair away from
him with the calves of his legs. He placed his
palms on each of the plank doors. There was
no other thought in his head but the one
thought he would never again, after this
night, need to hold onto.

To Thomas, it had been years since Pesty

had given the signal. His mind leaped and twisted. He tried to calculate how fast the Darrows were moving. He thought many times that they must have got by him. In another minute, he would have to yell out because of the exhaustion and excitement he felt. Then beside him stood a Darrow, when there had been nothing but trees a second before.

Thomas hadn't seen the Darrow come. He dared not move his head enough to see the man's trouser legs. But he knew the Darrow was there, standing in line with a tree. Standing so still, the Darrow could have been staring down at Thomas. Then he evaporated and went on. But this took minute upon minute. Thomas felt he would faint. He was suffocating, trying not to breathe out loud, when his insides ached for air and more air.

Once the Darrow had passed, Thomas couldn't help lifting his head and turning it quickly to the side. Fresh air hit him, cool and black. He breathed slowly and silently. He breathed so deeply, he thought he would explode.

There was another Darrow close to Thomas' father. Standing there, he was gone in a blink of Thomas' eye.

They are Mohegans, Thomas thought. We are Tuscaroras and they are Mohegans, not of our people.

He didn't see the third and last Darrow until the faint shape of him was in the clearing, close to where Mayhew lay. Next, all three forms were together and not moving. Thomas raised the lower part of his body upon his knees, keeping his head well down.

Darrows were whispering and looking around in all directions.

"I tell you he's gone, like they said," one was saying.

Another spoke quite clearly. "I don't like it—why ain't his torches burning on the cave?"

"Because he ain't here to light them, fool!"

"Mebbe so, but I can't see hardly a thing."

"When we get to the door, we can use the flashlight."

The forms moved slowly forward, ready to break away at the slightest sound. When they were about a foot in front of the cave, one of them turned on the flashlight.

Pluto slid himself out between the plank doors, blocking the Darrows before they had time to realize what had happened.

In the few minutes it had taken the Darrows to reach the cave, old Pluto had had an idea close to inspiration. Quickly bending down, he untied his shoes and removed the laces. Then, catching one end of his throw in his palm, he tied it to his wrist with a shoelace. When both ends of the throw were tied to both wrists, he pulled the neck of the throw behind his head, and fitted it over his top hat. What greeted the Darrows as they beamed their flashlight was a grotesque and chilling scene.

From the black mouth of the cave came an enormous bat with wings outstretched. By the time the Darrows realized it was Pluto, he was towering over them. With his arms held out to the height of his shoulders, he began to speak, his face turned toward the heavens.

"Come, my winged bird, my glory, night-bird! Come, all ye demons three who walk with me forever. Come parade awhile with Pluto, who has missed ye so!" His voice roared through the clearing. The Darrow men ducked down. One of them dropped the flashlight. When it hit the ground, it broke and went out.

In the trees on top of Mr. Pluto's cave, Pesty let drop the canvas sheet that had hidden the painted brilliance of Mr. Pluto's bay horse. Already mounted on the horse, she took a sure hold on each of the gossamer wings attached to his withers. As she dug her bare toes into the bay's flanks, she began to work the wings up and down.

What the Darrows saw was a glowing giant

of a thing, with wings as translucent as glimmering silk. The great wings brushed the air as lightly as feathers. The thing itself seemed to rise up and down, making only a muffled, soft sound.

There was a moan, as one Darrow sank down before the winged creature atop the cave.

Another one of them was yelling in a kind of strangled, husky scream.

The third and last began to jump up and down, first on one foot and then on the other.

The sight of the glowing bay with glimmering wings was indeed terrifying. Thomas, who was now supposed to come forward with Mr. Small and Mayhew, thus trapping the Darrows between ghosts and devils, was sagging down himself. He had not been prepared for the way Pluto looked, nor for the flashlight suddenly full on him. And no one had told him Pluto would say anything. Why had Pluto said what he had?

All at once Thomas was overcome with the night and with all the fear of Pluto that was buried deep inside him. He could not see Pesty on the bay's back. The reason he couldn't was that she was lying nearly flat, but Thomas didn't think of that. He simply saw that glowing devil of a horse and he began to sink down.

Mayhew grabbed hold of Thomas and carried him forward.

"Come to," he whispered. "We have got them. Stand up!"

Thomas stood, but barely. He and Mayhew and Mr. Small now spread themselves in a half circle behind the Darrows.

Just then, the Darrow who had fallen to his knees was lifted up by another Darrow and dragged away from the specter of Pluto and the winged demon, only to be dropped brutally at the sight of the three apparitions at the edge of the clearing. They shimmered so brightly that all three Darrows fell down.

All the Darrow men were yelling now. And Mayhew, as old Mr. Drear, was laughing in a most horrifying, crazed sound, screeching and groaning as he inched toward them. The laugh tore through what little courage Thomas had left, and he folded up again.

Mr. Small hissed at Thomas, rattling his chains and moaning so that Thomas would at least pump his arms, causing some of his own chains to clank.

The effect of Thomas' own fear was perhaps most convincing to the Darrows, for it seemed to them that he was a slave ghost still driven by invisible tormentors.

"Let me out of here!" one Darrow screamed.

"Mr. Pluto, Lordy, call 'em off. Call 'em off! Please, let me go! I won't come back, oh please!"

Mr. Pluto commenced to laugh. It was a deep, hateful sort of laugh, full of malice and memory of malice. He laughed and laughed. With his laughter, and Mayhew still screeching as Dies Drear, the whole hill rocked with the most earsplitting noise.

"Get them, my demons, get them!" cried Pluto.

Mr. Small raised his chains. So did Thomas. Mayhew folded his flowing arms around the closest Darrow.

Men were scrambling all over the clearing, Thomas got caught in his own chain and nearly broke his ankle; someone pulled him to his feet. He found himself face to face with a Darrow, and the Darrow was about ready to foam at the mouth. Suddenly all the Darrows broke away and were running free.

Mayhew began to laugh in his own voice. He slapped his hip and threw back his head and bellowed. One Darrow stopped dead in his tracks, just at the edge of the clearing where Thomas had been hiding. Mr. Pluto began to laugh, too, like a man who had successfully played a wonderful joke on someone. His was now a pleasant, healthy sort of laugh; he put his arm around Mayhew, folding him tenderly inside his throw. The Darrow stared at the two of them for the longest moment, then walked away.

When the Darrows had gone for sure, Mr. Small said, "You laughed too soon. The last one of them knew we were putting on for them."

"They would have figured it out, all of them, in another minute anyhow," Mayhew said. "The point is that for about fifteen seconds, we scared the living daylights out of them. And to make it worse, we laughed at them to their face because they allowed themselves to be fooled."

"You have to know Darrows," said old Pluto to Mr. Small. "It's bad enough that anybody would dare trick them. But to get away with that and then to laugh at 'em right in front of 'em, why they'll never live it down!"

"And they'll be about ready to pray we won't spread it around how we made fools out of them," Mayhew said. "I'm going to have Pesty tell them we let all the Carr boys watch!"

Mr. Small had to smile. "You are surely something," he said.

Then Mayhew and Pluto laughed and laughed.

Gently Mr. Small led Thomas into the cave. The boy was trembling all over. Mr. Small tried not to let Thomas know he had noticed.

Thomas was so ashamed. He would never be an actor. Never in a million years.

chapter 19

IN THE cavern of Dies Drear, Mr. Pluto sat behind his elaborate desk with a most satisfied grin upon his face.

Mr. Small and Thomas were tired out. They had changed from their slave costumes into their regular clothes. They'd finished removing the makeup and had piled their chains, wigs and such into a heap.

Pesty came in with the gossamer wings, which she placed on the very top of the heap. "I put the bay back in his stall," she said to Mayhew. "I cleaned the paint off him, too."

"You are a good baby," Mayhew said. "Now you ought to go to bed."

"Come here, Miss Bee," Pluto said to her. "Come sit on my lap. You know, you handled that horse and those wings just about perfect." He folded the smiling child within his throw, so that only her head, with eyes black and bright, peeked out.

"That was about the best show I've ever seen," Pluto said. "And you all wanted to put me in a hospital!"

"My mistake, Father," said Mayhew. He hadn't felt so friendly toward his father in a long time. "How in the name of heaven did you think up fixing that throw the way you did?"

"When you came out of that cave," said Mr. Small, "you looked like a huge, frightful bat."

"And what you said," Thomas said to old Pluto. He was still weak and trembling, and he wouldn't look at any of them. "You scared me, Mr. Pluto."

Mr. Pluto laughed softly. "It was a thrill for me," he said. "I had the best old time!"

Glancing at Thomas, Mayhew felt sorry for him. "Father did look pretty awful, what with that throw fixed the way it was. But being the way he is, I knew he would say something to terrify those Darrows. If I'm an actor at all, it's because he was one before me."

"I didn't do so well, did I?" Thomas said. "I guess I'm not too good as an actor." He couldn't find the words to apologize for his fear.

"You did just fine, son," said Mr. Small. "Having to lie there for so many hours—you did real well."

Thomas couldn't stand being treated so politely by them. He was growing angry at himself for being such a coward, and angry at them for being so nice about it.

"I think I'll go on home," he said. "See if Mama is sleeping."

"I'll walk over with you," Mayhew said. "Pesty, you ready to go over to Thomas' house and sleep?"

"She's asleep already," said Mr. Small. "Look."

It was true. Pesty had snuggled down against Mr. Pluto and was now fast asleep.

"Let her alone, Mayhew," Pluto said. "Mr. Small can take her home when he goes along—you will stay awhile, won't you, Mr. Small?" Mr. Small and old Pluto silently surveyed one another. Mr. Small nodded that he would stay.

"Why do you have to stay?" Thomas asked his father. "Why won't you come on home now?"

"Never you mind," said Mayhew. "Let's get going, see if we can find any more Darrows in the trees."

"There won't be any more Darrows," Thomas told him, "and I don't need you to walk me home."

"I'm not walking you home," said Mayhew. "I'm just going to walk with you, that's all. You don't want to be friends with me?"

Without Thomas becoming aware of it, Mayhew was leading him up the ramp and out of the cavern.

"I don't mind being friends," Thomas said. Secretly he was pleased that Mayhew had thought to go with him. "But I don't need anyone to take me home."

"I'm not taking you home, for pity's sake!" Mayhew said. "Man, you sure are a tough one to handle. How come you are so hard on people?"

"Well, I've always been independent," Thomas said seriously. "I make wood sculpture. I'm an artist, some say, and you have to be pretty much by yourself to be able to carve well." He felt full of pride when Mayhew looked at him with real interest.

"Wood sculpture? No kidding?"

"Sure," said Thomas. "I have even sold pieces to strangers. But mostly I just keep the pieces for myself and my family. Papa says I have a real talent for wood sculpture."

They went into Mr. Pluto's cave. The wall

of the cave slid across the opening, shutting off the cavern of Dies Drear.

In the cavern, Mr. Small stretched out on the floor to one side of Mr. Pluto's desk. He folded his arms across his chest and sighed deeply. Closing his tired eyes for a second, he opened them again to stare at the immense, vaulted ceiling far above his head.

"I think now you can tell me what this is all about," he said to Pluto. He was so tired, he would have no trouble falling asleep right where he was.

Mr. Pluto cleared his throat. "Mayhew said he would leave it to you," Pluto said. "Mayhew he told me this morning, whatever you said to do with this cavern was all right by him. And so I leave it up to you. I will trust you to do the right thing." Pluto tried to keep his voice casual, but deep within it was all his hope and his desire.

"I see," said Mr. Small. He sat up and fixed his gaze on the intricate, carved detail of the desk. "I was wondering a moment ago if anyone . . . Dies Drear, I mean, ever made a list of all the things in this cavern."

"No, not that I have found," Mr. Pluto said. "I have been through all the ledgers and books. I've found no list, nor no record of where he got any of it."

"Fascinating," said Mr. Small. "He never

ever meant any of it to be sold. And what a job to inventory all this. But I think I should, don't you? Give each piece a number, a name and description, and try to fix a value for it. What do you think, Mr. Skinner?" Mr. Small deliberately kept from looking at Pluto or around at the cavern.

And it was some time before Pluto spoke. Mr. Small was afraid he had fallen asleep, so still was he holding Pesty. But then Pluto breathed deeply.

"That will take as long as the rest of an old man's life," he said softly.

Mr. Small looked at him and smiled gently. "You know, sir, you have a way of saying things that I do admire," he said. "Your son, Mayhew, has the same gift with words. But just as you say, to inventory all this will take that long, at least."

"You will not turn this place over to the foundation right away?"

It was Mr. Small's turn to remain silent. When he did speak, it was with relief that at last he knew he had made up his mind. "All this has remained hidden for a century. Keeping it hidden awhile longer won't matter much." Saying this, Mr. Small felt peaceful inside.

Ever so carefully, Pluto got to his feet. "You take Miss Bee on home now," he said.

His old eyes looked mistily at the child.
"Just carry her like this, and she will sleep
all the way."

Mr. Small did as he was told. "I will begin
in the morning," he said. "I will inventory
the books and ledgers first."

"They'll be ready," said Pluto. "Come as
early as you will."

That was all then. Mr. Small left, carrying
Pesty through the trees as carefully as old
Pluto would have. Part way home, he passed
close to someone he could but barely see.
There was a laugh, a deep, sharp sound in
the pine boughs. It was Mayhew coming
back. He didn't stop to speak, nor did Mr.
Small.

A half hour before, Thomas and Mayhew
had gone through the trees all the way home.
Thomas wouldn't have believed they could
become friends so quickly.

"You can learn a lot about acting in the
month I'll be here," Mayhew had said.

"You mean you will teach me?"

"I can teach you a good amount if you
think you really want to learn," Mayhew said.

"I don't think I'd be much good at it,"
said Thomas. "But there's one thing I've seen
you do that I'd like to learn."

"What's that?"

"How is it you can seem to flow out of

doorways," Thomas asked, "like you were liquid spilling into the night? How do you do that, Mayhew?"

Mayhew laughed. "I'll have to think about that one. Maybe I can break it down and show you." He laughed again, and they walked without speaking.

"You know," Mayhew said suddenly, "I'm glad we did what we did tonight. Not so much scaring the Darrows. That was important, too, because now they know they can never fool with your father the way they did with mine. They'll fear your father in a way they never feared mine. They'll fear him not as a devil but as a man. He will have the right to say who can pass here and who cannot. Yes, they'll be afraid of him and the law he won't hesitate to use against them.

"But what I meant to say about being glad is that my father had such a good time with it. I felt closer to him tonight than I think I ever have."

"You never liked him much?" Thomas asked. He felt he could ask that. He felt Mayhew wouldn't mind talking about it.

"No, I never did," Mayhew said. "It's hard for a boy growing up without his father, not even able to wish for him since he didn't like him to begin with. You like your father though, don't you, Thomas?"

"Sometimes I get angry with him," Thomas said. "He always has to figure out everything before I do. Like in the house when we were planning to scare the Darrows."

Mayhew smiled. "Your father knew we were going to too much trouble to be scaring just plain people."

"No," said Thomas, "he had a report from the foundation about the whole history of the house, and from it he must have figured out that the third slave and you and your father and the Darrows were all mixed up together.

"But sure, I like him fine. He's pretty smart, you know. Folks always did say he had a powerful brain."

Mayhew laughed softly.

Then Thomas said, "Do you suppose I and that youngest Darrow, that Mac Darrow, do you think we could get to be friends?"

"Oh well," Mayhew said, "the Darrows aren't going to want him or Pesty fooling around here for a very long time. And you have to remember, Macky's a Darrow after all—we did fool his brothers pretty bad. He has to live it down, too, you know. But give it time. Anger might die down by the change of a couple of seasons. Wait for the winter. You'll most likely run into Macky here in these trees full of snow, when you both are out hunting rabbit."

"It will take that long a time?" Thomas said.

"That's not a long time. When you begin to think it is, just remember Father hunting thirty years for his legacy, which might have never existed. Yes, winter will be here before you have got to know this land properly. You will feel and breathe an air so cold that all things holding warmth will be your friend."

"You love it here," Thomas said. "How come you go away from it?"

"That's my secret, my friend," said Mayhew. "Not all questions can have answers to be said out loud."

They had entered Thomas' house. Mrs. Small was asleep on the couch in the parlor. On the floor beside the couch was Thomas' baseball bat.

"I'll be going," Mayhew whispered again. "I won't see you tomorrow. I have to take care of business in Dayton. I'll see you the next day though, and we will maybe start your stage lessons."

Thomas said good night to him. He didn't wake Mrs. Small, but went up to his own room. He didn't even bother about the captain's chair, which still sat with its back to the room. There were his carvings, so familiar, grouped on the mantelpiece. Falling across his bed, he was instantly asleep.

Thomas awoke about ten o'clock the next morning. His clothing was hardly wrinkled, but he was stiff in every muscle. He washed his face, brushed his teeth and combed his hair. Not bothering to change his shirt, he went quickly down the hall and down the stairs. He found his mother busy with the twins in the kitchen. She looked tired, but she smiled at Thomas pleasantly and fixed him a heaping plate of ham and eggs with potatoes. Thomas ate all of it in a few minutes. He had two glasses of milk and two slices of toast besides.

"You were hungry, for sure," Mrs. Small said.

"Did Papa tell you about last night?" Thomas asked. "Did he tell you how we did it?"

"He told me," she said. "I'm glad I wasn't there. I wouldn't have been able to go through with it. Every time I think of you lying out there for so long, and little Pesty on that big horse, I can't believe it."

"It was really something," Thomas said. "We scared those Darrows half to death." He had forgotten about his own fear.

"Where is Papa anyway?" he asked. He didn't think to inquire after Pesty.

"Over at the cavern," Mrs. Small said.

Thomas kissed his brothers. "Boys, you like this big, old house of Smalls? You going to get lost in it and cause me worry? Maybe I'll take you hunting when winter snow falls, would you like that?"

The boys grinned happily at Thomas.

"I'm going to see Papa," said Thomas to Mrs. Small.

"Tell him I expect him back here about eleven," she said. "He went out after having only a half cup of coffee. And he will have to take you to register for school sometime. He's got an appointment at one to see someone at the college. And later on I would like to see that cavern myself. You tell him now, Thomas."

Thomas went. The morning was fine and clear and the trees on the hill as he went through them were fresh with dew. In no time he was over the hill and in Mr. Pluto's cave. Inside the cave there was a ringing, pounding noise going on. It was a noise of metal beating against metal. Thomas walked the short tunnel to the main cave. A great fire roared in Mr. Pluto's forge. Every once in awhile Mr. Pluto turned to work his bellows. Then Pluto would hammer on white-hot metal, held over the fire. He paused a moment as Thomas came close.

"What are you doing?" Thomas asked him. Mr. Pluto was dripping wet but otherwise looked strong and healthy.

"I'm making me the biggest lock you ever did see," he said. "And good morning to you."

"Good morning," said Thomas. "What for?"

Pluto beat and turned the white-hot metal. "For to lock good those plank doors you just came through."

"You never locked them before," said Thomas.

"I know it," Pluto answered him.

"Well, you surely don't need to lock them now," Thomas said.

"I know that, too," old Pluto said, "but I think I will just the same. I haven't had something to do in so long!" He beat and turned the metal that now took shape. Thomas stared at him with his mouth open. A grin spread across his face. Then he asked if it were all right to go into the cavern. Mr. Pluto said for him to go right ahead.

Thomas walked to the wall where the rope was. He pulled down on that rope and watched the wall slide back.

Within the cavern the wall slid closed behind Thomas. He took his time going through the stalagmites. He walked around them to touch them, feeling the damp coolness of them. Far below sat his father at Mr. Pluto's desk. Mr. Small worked furiously on long sheets of yellow paper. He had books and ledgers from the cases piled on the floor around him. Thomas went down the ramp, taking his time. Finally he stood before his father.

Mr. Small sneezed and coughed. His nose was running. He glanced up at Thomas and nodded a hurried greeting. "Listing everything . . ." he said. He shook his head. "There is so much! This is only the beginning. And it makes fine reading . . . I have to read it, don't I? It will take me years!"

"Is that what you're going to do? List every bit and piece of it?" Thomas asked.

Mr. Small stopped long enough to blow his nose. "Well, we have to know how much there is," he said. "Since we don't know where Drear got it all, we can at least make a record of what it is. If the foundation is to have any order, if it should wish to start a museum . . ." He folded his handkerchief and began to read to himself from some volume that looked to Thomas as though it would fall into dust at any moment.

"Papa . . ." Thomas said.

"Shhh. Thomas, there is so much to do. Years!"

Thomas told him what Mrs. Small had said.

"Yes, yes," was all Mr. Small answered. Thomas couldn't tell if his father had listened or not.

Mr. Pluto's brown throw was lying on the floor by some books. Thomas went around, picked it up and carefully put it around his father's shoulders.

"You caught yourself a cold," he said softly. "You'd better take care."

Mr. Small continued reading. Once he smiled vaguely at Thomas, not unkindly. But his eyes were full of the eager concern he had for the work ahead of him.

It was then Thomas saw Pesty sitting at the very top of the ladder, next to the shelves of bottles. She had a cloth in her hand; she smiled at Thomas and held out the cloth. Thomas placed a finger to his lips and shook his head. He held out his arms to her. Pesty came halfway down the ladder and Thomas lifted her the rest of the way. He went up the ladder and seated himself at the top. Again he held out his arms for Pesty. She climbed up and sat a few rungs below him.

"Papa's going to work himself until he catches the flu," he whispered in Pesty's ear.

"If he gets sick," she whispered back, "you'll have to give him the medicine, like I do for Mr. Pluto."

They sat for a long time then, without saying anything. Pesty was content to sit with Thomas, and Thomas by now was used to having her around.

Looking at the cavern from high up was different than seeing it down below. Suddenly Thomas saw the thick chain almost hidden by bright tapestries. He had noticed it the first time he and Mr. Small had entered the cavern. Now he could tell what was at the end of it. He pointed at it for Pesty. She nodded.

"It's been up there forever," she whispered.

High up, the chain was looped on a thick hook projected from the ceiling. Hanging from the end of the chain was a black trunk. It was quite a large trunk, which bulged with something that would one day burst its seams.

Thomas' curiosity was aroused. But then he leaned back. Slowly it came to him that he didn't care at all what was in the trunk. In the vastness of the cavern, one more item didn't seem to matter.

Let it stay a mystery, he thought. As long as the chain and hook can hold it, just let it stay there.

He didn't bother to look at it or to think about it again.

He and Pesty sat watching the still form

of Mr. Small, almost hidden beneath Mr. Pluto's throw. They would wait for as long as they had to. They would wait on the ladder by the bottles as long as it would take Mr. Small to remind himself of them and need them to help. And they didn't mind the waiting, not this day nor the days to come. They had years.

ABOUT THE AUTHOR

VIRGINIA HAMILTON grew up in Yellow Springs, Ohio, a southern Ohio community similar to the one Thomas moves to in *The House of Dies Drear*. This rural area of villages and farms was an important network on the Underground Railroad system to Canada during the Civil War era. As a child, Miss Hamilton was aware that many of the large old houses in her own community had once concealed running slaves. Her ancestors were among the one hundred thousand slaves who fled from the South in the first half of the nineteenth century, forty thousand of whom are said to have passed through Ohio.

Miss Hamilton believes her books grow out of her childhood wonder about these fleeing people. "I had a longing as a child," she has said. "I needed to know how men, women and children could travel hundreds of miles on foot through enemy land. I found out that they were brave and clever almost beyond belief. Perhaps with this book I have at last touched them the way they first touched me so long ago."

As far back as she can remember, Miss Hamilton says, she has wanted to be a writer. "I never thought seriously of any other career." She attended Antioch College and the Ohio State University. After living in New York for many years, she recently moved back to Yellow Springs with her husband and children.